# LOVES ME, LOVES ME NOT

An IN or OUT Novel

**BY CLAUDIA GABEL**

IN or OUT

LOVES ME, LOVES ME NOT
An IN or OUT Novel

SWEET AND VICIOUS
An IN or OUT Novel

# LOVES ME

## LOVES ME NOT

**An In or Out Novel by**

# CLAUDIA GABEL

*Point*

ISBN-13: 978-0-439-91854-1
ISBN-10: 0-439-91854-5

Copyright © 2007 by Claudia Gabel
All rights reserved. Published by Scholastic Inc.

SCHOLASTIC and associated logos are trademarks and/or registered trademarks of Scholastic Inc.

Text design by Steve Scott
The text type was set in Bulmer.

12 11 10 9 8 7 6 5 4 3 2 1                    7 8 9 10 11 12/0

Printed in the U.S.A.
First printing, September 2007

For the Gloucester Girls — Erin, Julianna, Kim, and Michelle

# Chapter 1

Marnie Fitzpatrick flinched when she heard the dismissal bell ringing loudly in her ears. It was 2:57 P.M. on the day when she and her best friend, Nola James, had their first fight — not the average "I can't believe you lost my favorite cashmere scarf!" type of fight (which would have been bad enough), but a colossal, volcanic, "If I *ever* see you again, I will scratch your eyes out *and* spit in your face!" type of fight.

As her classmates filed out of the room one by one, Marnie gripped her Earth Science textbook and took a deep breath. *Posture,* she said to herself. *Think strong, confident posture.* She rolled her head forward and touched her chin to her chest, then rolled her head back until she heard her neck make a small cracking noise. Then she loosened her shoulders and brought them back so she wasn't slouching. When she was finished with her relaxation routine, Marnie grabbed her things and stood up, remembering to smooth out her black-and-red pleated plaid miniskirt and adjust the barrette fastened in her wavy blonde hair.

Even though she'd been on edge all day, Marnie knew she had to look cool and composed once she walked out of this room. Everyone in school was still whispering and gossiping about her and Nola's show-down. If Marnie's older sister, Erin, were here, she'd remind Marnie that she couldn't risk losing the stellar reputation she had built at her birthday party two days ago. So no matter what happened from here on out, Marnie had one resolve — to show that her newly found almost-a-Major (a.k.a. popular) status was well deserved and hard-earned, not a fluke.

With her books cradled in the nook of her right arm and her tote bag held tightly in her left hand, Marnie strolled down the hall toward her locker. She weaved through the crowd and smiled when she realized that her classmates were watching her walk by in admiration, as if she owned Poughkeepsie Central and every other high school in the district.

*Wow, maybe I should get into fights in public more often,* she thought.

When Marnie opened her locker, her grin became even wider. There was a cute little sketch of a stick figure doing a yoga pose hanging up on the inside of her locker. A message from a friend was written on it in neat, yet bubbly cursive.

*Yoga, baby! After school. No excuses!*

Marnie laughed as she took the sign down, folded it up, and put it in her bag with her homework. If it hadn't been for Lizette Levin, Poughkeepsie Central's most sought-after freshman girl, Marnie would have been a complete mess today. Lizette saw to it that Marnie didn't spend one minute regretting what happened with Nola. In fact, when Marnie explained to Lizette what their argument had been about during lunch, Lizette had blown Marnie away with her response.

"Nola's just jealous of you, Marn. Don't sweat that girl because she's, like, insecure."

Those words had given Marnie comfort all afternoon, and now this note proved she was a permanent part of Lizette's fabu inner circle. What could be better than that?

Marnie spun around when she felt a tiny pinch on her side.

"Hey," Lizette said, casually leaning against the locker next to Marnie's. Her hair was up in a sleek, sophisticated high ponytail, and her lips were freshly glossed.

"Hi, Zee." During lunch today, Lizette had also told Marnie to call her by her nickname, which only close friends, other Majors, and hotties were allowed to use.

"Are you ready to get in touch with your Zen?" Lizette asked.

Marnie checked her watch. She was supposed to be at the bus stop in a few minutes. Her heart started racing at the thought of the ride home with Nola. All the tension and awkwardness that Marnie had experienced when her parents were fighting right before their divorce would be back for an encore performance if she was forced to have another showdown with Nola behind the bus driver's back. An escape plan sounded perfect.

"Yeah, it sounds like fun," Marnie replied cheerily.

Lizette reached into her pocket, pulled out a tin of sour apple Altoids, and popped one in her mouth. "Awesome. It'll, like, totally transform your body."

Marnie felt a twinge of nervousness in her stomach. Unbeknownst to anyone but Nola, although Marnie stretched a little before each of her runs, she had the flexibility of a brick. A vision of her attempting a simple pose, falling on her butt, and humiliating herself flashed into her mind. Suddenly, the bus ride with Nola was looking pretty good.

"Actually, now that I think about it, I have a *ton* of homework to do. I really should go straight home," Marnie said, closing her locker and hoisting her bag up onto her shoulder.

"It's only an hour class. Come on, it'll be fun," Lizette pleaded.

Marnie giggled when Lizette resorted to sad puppy-dog eyes. "Okay, okay. Let's go."

"Omigod, you are going to *love* it!" Lizette said while taking Marnie's hand and pulling her friend toward the front door.

Marnie looked down and saw Nola's stylish, funky bracelet dangling off Lizette's wrist. Immediately, she remembered the angry and hurt expression on Nola's face and the tears in Nola's eyes when they were at each other's throats in the hallway. It was enough to make Marnie stop and catch her breath before she trotted down the front steps with Lizette.

When they reached the parking lot, Lizette broke away and dashed over to her father's SUV while Marnie lagged behind, wondering if Lizette was ever going to give the bracelet back. And if she didn't, whether or not Marnie would care.

"Now, without lifting up the balls of your feet, stretch forward, reach out, and press the palms of your hands on the mat."

When the lithe female instructor at Arlington Yoga-Works said these words, the first thought in Marnie's head was, *Say* what? If she leaned over in this manner, everyone in the row behind her would get to see her bright yellow GapBody underwear sticking out of the black low-rise yoga pants that Lizette had lent her. And then there was the problem of not being able to bend down and touch her ankles, let alone her feet *or* the mat that was beneath them. She couldn't have been more frustrated.

Marnie quickly glanced over at Lizette, who already had her hands placed on the ground. Marnie marveled not only at how limber Lizette was, but how chic she looked — Lizette was wearing these super-cute marmalade-colored cropped gaucho pants and a graphic-print tank top turned inside out. She'd even styled her hair into two braided pigtails. She was adorable *and* the balls of her feet were still on the ground!

Suddenly, a voice startled Marnie.

"Are you having trouble, dear?" the instructor asked from the front of the classroom. She was middle-aged, had clearly colored her hair with Nice 'n Easy #113 A, and had obviously worked as a circus contortionist in her youth.

Marnie cleared her throat. "Oh, no. I'm just . . . breathing."

"Breathing is good! In and out, along with the movements," Ms. Cirque du Soleil said as she fluidly went into the next pose.

Marnie tried to appease the instructor by leaning forward so she was creating a right angle with her body.

But that was as low as she was willing to go. She was afraid her boobs might pop out of the V-neck T-shirt that Lizette had given her, and she'd had enough drama for the day.

The instructor came back to a standing position. Marnie was in awe of her posture. "Okay, let's take a short break before we begin the advanced portion of our workout."

*Advanced?*

"So what do you think? She's really fierce, huh?" Lizette's cheeks were rosy and her skin was glistening.

"She sure is," Marnie said, swallowing hard. "I *loved* that one move of hers — the five-pointed star."

Lizette laughed. "You mean the one where you stand with your legs spread apart and your arms out to your sides?"

"Um, yeah." Marnie could feel herself blushing. The pose was so simple it could be done by a two-year-old, a two-hundred-year-old, or anyone in between.

"Well, I'm glad you're challenging yourself," Lizette said with a playful nudge.

It was strange — a few days ago, Marnie would have been frantic at the thought of Lizette perceiving her as uncool, but now she was able to giggle at Lizette's sarcasm, just like a true friend would.

They strolled over to the water fountain, and Marnie grabbed a paper cup, filled one to the top, and handed it to Lizette.

"So are you excited about the election?" Lizette asked before taking a sip of her water.

Even after all of today's turmoil, Marnie couldn't help but smile when she thought of the upcoming class elections. At first, Marnie had been a little worried that only the hard-core Leeks ran for office (with the exception of Dane Harris, who Marnie thought defied all categorization). But ever since Lizette had likened winning a spot on student government to dominating the high-school social order, Marnie immediately stopped worrying and got psyched.

"I'm way excited, especially because Dane offered to coach me on my leadership skills," Marnie said, blushing.

*Dane, beautiful Dane.* Marnie thought back to yesterday's touch-football game at Bartlett Park. Dane had looked so perfect in his gray hooded sweatshirt, with his blond hair tousled and grass stains on his pants. She recalled their last kiss and how soft his lips were and how he'd reached down and squeezed her butt a little. She had to pound her paper cup of water to prevent herself from hyperventilating.

"Leadership skills? Oh, please." Lizette giggled,

tossed her cup in the trash, and led Marnie back to the center of the room. "Honestly, Marnie, from what I hear, that boy worships you as much as Sawyer worships me. Like, maybe even *more*."

"Are you serious?" Marnie asked. It was a little weird to hear that her own former crush/skater king Sawyer Lee was worshipping anyone else but her. Still, Marnie's heart performed a flying-trapezelike leap at the thought of Dane building a shrine in her honor.

"I'm *always* serious about boys," Lizette added with a wink. "As for the election, with Dane as your — ahem — 'coach' and me as your campaign manager, you're going to win by a landslide."

Marnie was so ecstatic she nearly did a half lotus fold (whatever that was). "Omigod, *you'd* be my campaign manager? That would be awesome!"

Lizette's smile glowed. "I know."

Marnie felt as though she owed every bit of happiness she'd experienced in the last two weeks to Lizette, and when Marnie looked into the future, she was sure Lizette would be the source of all the happiness that was to come.

"Okay, now let me help you with that pose we just did," Lizette said.

"I'm in your hands."

Marnie took a deep breath, in and out, and poorly imitated every one of Lizette's graceful movements. But she thought to herself that one day, with lots of practice, they'd be as graceful as her friend's, yet all her own.

# Chapter 2

As Nola James boarded one of Poughkeepsie Central's brand-new yellow school buses, she was 100 percent convinced that she was suffering from a severe case of post-traumatic stress disorder. Not only was she sweating like she had scarlet fever, but she was getting increasingly dizzy as she climbed each step and walked down the long aisle toward the back of the bus.

Her knees buckled when she fell into one of the olive-green leather seats, clutching her bag tightly on her lap. Nola swallowed hard and tried not to look up, because if she did, she might get a glimpse of Marnie, and then everything about this morning would come back to her like a vivid nightmare.

Nola had relived those few minutes in her mind hundreds of times over the course of the day. She remembered how Marnie had snapped at her before homeroom, how Lizette walked in wearing the bracelet Nola had made for Marnie's birthday, and how Marnie was unapologetic when Nola confronted her about it. The thought of Marnie's coldness made Nola especially nauseous. Why wasn't Marnie even the least bit sorry for betraying her like that? And then memories from the past two weeks had come rolling in like twenty-foot waves — the botched plans, the unreturned calls, the promises broken. She was tearing up so badly that she had to wipe her eyes with the sleeve of her favorite orange-and-red striped Billabong Henley.

More of Nola's classmates got on the bus, and she buried her head in her hands so she wouldn't make eye contact with them. All day long, she had tried not to let her blowout with Marnie affect her, but her efforts had meant nothing. She had been way too distracted to pay attention to simple things, like walking (she tripped up the same flight of stairs — *twice* in two hours), sitting (she somehow slipped out of her seat in Tech class and took the desk down with her), eating (in the cafeteria, she dropped a can of Coke onto her book bag), and listening (her Advanced Freshman Physics teacher Mr. Newkirk asked her a question about vectors and her reply was "Constantinople").

If Marnie got on this bus, Nola's life was only going to get worse, and quite frankly, she had a hunch that a horrendous case of hives — an unfortunate chronic condition of hers — would consume her whole.

"Can I sit here?" A cheery, upbeat voice drifted into Nola's ear.

Slowly, Nola brought her face out from behind her hands and glanced up. Iris Santos was greeting her with a smirk and her signature head shake/bangs fling, which revealed her dark yet shining eyes.

Nola nodded her head and scooted over toward the window.

"Crappy day, huh?" Iris said.

Nola sighed heavily. "You could say that again."

"Crappy day, huh? Sorry! I couldn't resist."

But Nola was in no mood for Iris's jokes. In fact, Nola wondered what Iris was doing on the bus in the first place. Usually, Iris had debate team after school, and then her mom would pick her up. "How come you're not at practice?" Nola asked.

"Oh, Mrs. Wasserman flaked out because her husband got her tickets to see some sort of poor man's *Stars on Ice* show at the Civic Center." Iris rolled her eyes and crossed her arms over her chest defiantly. "The woman does *not* represent. I can't respect that."

Nola could only manage a half-smile.

"But enough about me. How are you holding up, girl?"

"I'm . . . okay," Nola mumbled.

"Yeah. Right. And I'm soft-spoken and shy," Iris said with a snicker. "Listen, Marnie is going to realize how bogus those chicks are one day, she will."

Nola could tell that Iris was trying to make her feel

better, but it wasn't working. Still, she was happy she had someone to lean on if Marnie got on the bus, which could happen any second now.

All of a sudden there was a *tap-tap-tap*! on the glass.

"Oh, my god!" Nola's breath caught in her throat.

She looked out the window and there stood Matt Heatherly. One of his hands was on the handlebar of his bike and the other one was in the air, waving hello. In an instant, Nola's emotions went from tortured to euphoric. Matt looked amazing. His hair was uncombed (as per usual), his faded jeans were falling down a little, and the cuffs on his beat-up Army jacket were rolled up once, so she could see his blue wristband.

And in the next instant, Nola was thrown back to tortured status.

*Riley Finnegan*, she thought. *He has a girlfriend named Riley Finnegan.*

Iris stood up on the seat, leaned over Nola, and opened the window. "Whaddya want, peon?" she shouted at eardrum-shattering volume.

"You still mad about the other day?" Matt smiled, and then broke into a laugh. "I'm sorry our hot date was a wash, okay? But I'm afraid I'm taken."

Nola's stomach churned so hard she thought she might double over in pain.

"That is one *desperate* female," Iris said, tossing her hair with attitude.

Matt shook his head. "Iris, just tell Nola to come out here."

"Tell her your damn self!" And with that, Iris slammed the window shut and sat back down.

Nola saw Matt smirking at her, and she couldn't help but smile back. He gestured with his head, beckoning her to meet him outside. Nola looked back at Iris, who was chuckling to herself.

"By all means, Nola, go on ahead." Iris got up and cleared a path for her.

"Thanks." Nola grabbed her things and made her way down the aisle. As she descended the steps, Matt rolled his bike over to welcome her.

"Hey," he said.

Nola swallowed hard. "Hey."

"I wanted to know if you needed a lift home."

"Um, Matt, in case you didn't notice, I was on *the bus*."

Matt scratched his head. "Yeah, good point."

Nola knew what he was up to, though. He was checking on her to see if she was okay. How sweet was that?

"Still, the bus is so . . . old-fashioned, don't you

think? Wouldn't you rather see the greater Poughkeepsie region on the seat of a bike, driven by a retired paper-boy?" Matt patted the vinyl seat with his large, perfect hands.

Nola's horrible day was fading away from her thoughts. So much so, that she found it easy to joke with Matt. "I think I'd rather live to see fourteen."

"I turned fourteen over the summer. Don't believe the hype," he said, grinning.

Nola laughed. Everything was easy with him. *Everything*.

"Come on, you know you want to," Matt teased. "And this is a one-time offer. You snooze, you lose."

Nola could hardly argue with him. She did want to sit on that bike and hold on to Matt's waist for dear life. She did want him to give her an escape route — the bus was going to leave soon, and Marnie was sure to come dashing out of the back doors to where the buses were lined up for departure. Nola did want Matt to make her forget about her terrible day and all the terrible days that were ahead. But more than anything, Nola wanted to forget that Riley Finnegan ever existed. Then it dawned on her that if she accepted this bike ride, maybe, possibly, Matt might forget Riley existed, too.

"Just don't pull any crazy stunts, all right?" Nola said as she approached him cautiously.

Matt took his free hand and patted her gently on the back. "I promise, Nola, I would never do anything to hurt you."

When Matt pedaled off with Nola grabbing him around his waist and her legs dangling off the sides, she asked herself if she could ever believe in promises again.

She would have to wait and see.

"You promised no stunts!" Nola screamed as Matt wove his way through traffic down Mill Street. "Slow down!"

She couldn't see Matt's face, but she could tell that he was laughing his head off. "This isn't a stunt, Nol! And I'm not even going that fast."

Nola involuntarily clutched Matt's waist when he jerked his bike to the left so he could pass a cobalt blue Volkswagen Bug. "Why can't we ride on the sidewalk?" she asked.

"Why can't you stop digging your fingernails into my flesh?" Matt shouted over the street noise, trying to wriggle out of Nola's death grip. "Just calm down and enjoy the scenery, okay?"

Nola whipped her head to the left, then to the right. The only things visible on Mill Street were storefronts and lots of cars speeding past them. How typically lame and boring of Poughkeepsie. "*What* scenery?" she bellowed.

But Matt just ignored her and picked up the pace, abruptly turning onto Academy Street and missing a mail truck by a few inches. Nola grabbed Matt even harder and screeched at the top of her lungs.

"*Oooowwww!*" Matt roared, almost losing control of the bike. "God, Nola! Are you trying to draw blood?"

"Sorry!" she shrieked. Only a few more blocks and this insanity would all be over. Nola closed her eyes tightly and prayed that they'd reach their destination in one piece.

Thankfully, her prayers were answered.

Minutes later, Matt's bike skid to a stop in front of Nola's large Victorian house on Winding Way, with both passenger and driver fully intact. Nola got off the seat slowly and wobbled over to the porch, where she sat down on the steps in complete exhaustion.

*I should have taken the bus.*

Matt released the kickstand with his foot and parked his bike on the lawn. Then he walked toward Nola, wincing and rubbing his sides. "Is Doctor Mom home? I think I have internal injuries that need immediate surgery."

Nola rolled her eyes. "That's what you get for driving like a maniac. How you survived your paper route is beyond me."

"What can I say? I'm a daredevil." Matt sat down next to Nola and leaned back so that his elbows were resting on the porch. His T-shirt pulled up a little, revealing the lower part of his stomach and half of his belly button. "One day, you'll learn to love that about me."

Nola was, quite literally, gasping for air.

"So . . . are you going to tell me what happened between you and Marnie this morning?" Matt's gaze was piercing right through Nola's Henley and into her heart. "You didn't say a word at lunch, or during Physics."

"It's a long story." Nola stared hard at her mailbox at the edge of the curb. She could feel her eyes welling up with tears at the memory of a nine-year-old Marnie putting a plate of peanut-butter chocolate-chip cookies in it when Nola had an ear infection. The note had read, "Hope these cookies are *DEF*!" but the play on words had gone right over Nola's head.

"Well, I'm guessing it had something to do with Lizette," Matt said, leaning forward so that he could meet Nola's gaze.

Nola's skin became itchy at the mere mention of Lizette Levin's name. "What makes you say that?"

"Um, nothing really, except for the way your eyes rolled back in your head and steam came out of your ears when she showed up for homeroom." Matt nudged Nola lightly with his knee. "You sure you don't want to talk about it?"

Nola turned her head and looked right at Matt. She smiled as she studied the sharp angles of his jawline and the round curve of his earlobes and his thin, slightly pink lips, all of which Riley Finnegan had probably kissed a hundred times. Nola's heart went into a fit of spasms.

"She was wearing the bracelet," Nola finally said, shivering. A crisp fall breeze had just washed over her.

"Wait, are we talking about the bracelet you made for Marnie as a birthday gift?"

Nola nodded solemnly.

"Wow," he said, stunned. "That's . . . really messed up."

"I know. I just saw it on Lizette and completely lost my mind. Maybe shouting at Marnie wasn't the right thing to do," she said, biting her lower lip.

Matt shifted a little so the right side of his body was just touching the left side of Nola's. "You lost your temper. So what? It happens to the best of us, and if it ends your friendship, then maybe that friendship wasn't so great to begin with."

Matt's words blindsided Nola. Maybe he had a point. Nola rarely got angry with Marnie and this time she had a right to be. If Marnie couldn't handle it, then perhaps it was best they went their separate ways. But as soon as that thought crossed her mind, Nola could feel her bottom lip trembling.

"I . . . I'm just going to miss her, that's all," Nola said, tearing up again. "I told her everything, you know? I talked to her at least ten times a day. And now we're not speaking *at all.*"

Matt put a consoling arm around Nola's shoulders and pulled her in for a half-hug. She couldn't help but take a deep breath and inhale — *mmmm, Bounce with Febreze fabric softener.*

"Okay, I think I have a solution to your problem," he said.

Nola gulped. "You do?"

"I'm willing to bet that you and Marnie are going to make up in a week, two weeks tops," Matt said confidently. "But until you do, you need the equivalent of a best-friend patch to get you through your Marnie withdrawal. Are you with me?"

It was as if she were reading Marnie's ear-infection note for the first time. "Not really."

Matt chuckled. "Let me put it another way. *I* can be your best friend understudy. I'll stand in and play the role of Marnie until the two of you work things out. What do you think?"

Nola sat there, frozen like a snowcap. Matt was offering to be her *temporary best friend*. That meant a lot more talking, a lot more hanging out together, a lot more almost-flirting.

There was just one problem, and her initials were *RF*. The more time Nola spent with Matt, the more she'd have to hear about his girlfriend, and it was already excruciatingly painful just knowing Riley was on MySpace, blogging her way into Matt's heart each day.

She had to think this through.

"It's so nice of you to offer, but —"

"Don't worry, you can mull it over," Matt said, holding up a hand to indicate that she didn't have to say anything else. Then he stood, stretched, and swaggered over to his bike.

"I will, thanks." Nola practically had to clench her whole body into a ball to prevent herself from running up and hugging him.

He swung his left leg over his bike and perched himself on the seat. "See ya tomorrow, Nola."

"See ya," she replied, not taking her eyes off of him for a second as he pedaled down the sidewalk, as careful as a temporary best friend should be.

# Chapter 3

THIS WEEK'S TO-DO LIST

1. Buy large fluorescent flash cards at Staples for pre-election speech. Get new pens, too.
2. SHOP FOR OUTFIT TO WEAR TO THE ASSEMBLY! Something that says, "I'm brainy, yet bubbly!" Perhaps a wrap dress from Express?
3. Stop slacking off on morning runs. Missing two days in a row is not acceptable.
4. Convince Mom to turn Erin's room into something useful like a game room or a huge closet. She can sleep on the pull-out couch when she comes home from PENN, can't she?
5. AVOID NOLA AT ALL COSTS!

On Tuesday morning in homeroom, Marnie's posture was about as straight as a hunchback's. She rubbed at the sore spot behind her right shoulder with her left hand, but it was no use. Marnie had strained one of her muscles while attempting the Reverse Warrior pose, which Lizette had said would help improve the flow of her chi. Or was it to channel her yang? Marnie couldn't remember which, *or* turn her neck to the side without wincing.

But it had all been worth it. After they left Arlington YogaWorks, Marnie and Lizette had spent a couple of hours eating vegetarian deluxe pizza at Gino's, talking about boys and clothes, and going over preliminary election strategies. Marnie's excitement was now at its peak. As Lizette picked the olives off her slice, she'd explained how previous Majors before them, including former senior-class secretary Erin Fitzpatrick, had taken charge of the school by staying true to this simple philosophy: "If you *make* the rules, you can *break* the rules."

Marnie really liked the sound of this mantra. Up until recently, she hadn't been much of a rule maker — she was always looking to Erin for cues on how to behave and what to do. Hanging out with Nola for eight years didn't help Marnie in the rule-breaker department, either. Nola had way too much nervous energy to do anything risky, and Marnie could never trust her former best friend to stay calm in a precarious situation, especially that one time when . . .

"So, I hear that you and Lizette went to YogaWorks after school yesterday."

If Marnie had the ability to look over her right shoulder, she would have seen that Brynne Callaway was addressing her. However, Marnie could recognize Brynne by the extra-snotty cadence of her voice. She slowly shifted in her seat so that she could greet Brynne's smug-looking face, gap-toothed grin, and clingy-as-Saran-Wrap wardrobe, which included a short denim skirt that she kept tugging on at the hem.

"You heard right," Marnie said over the noise of morning announcements.

Brynne rolled her eyes and threw Marnie a nasty glare. "*I'm* supposed to have Mondays."

Marnie was confused. Was there a schedule she didn't know about? "What do you mean you have Mondays?"

"It's called QT," Brynne huffed. *"Quality time?"*

"I know what QT stands for, okay?" Marnie barked, even though she'd had no idea.

"What*ever*," Brynne said through pursed lips. "Just *don't* let it happen again."

Marnie's head snapped back in disbelief. *Is she actually threatening me? Over who gets Mondays?*

As she tried to think up a comeback, Marnie couldn't help but take notice of the deep, lilting, sexy-as-hell voice coming over the intercom, which belonged to Dane Harris. He was reminding everyone about important election dates — next Thursday would be the nominee speeches; voting would occur the following day and be tallied over the weekend; and the winners would be revealed two Mondays from now.

But even Dane's smooth-as-satin vocals couldn't calm Marnie down.

Marnie narrowed her eyes at Brynne. She wasn't going to take this girl's attitude any longer. She opened her mouth and prepared to grill Brynne with some "take *that!*" comment. But then —

*Marnie Fitzpatrick, please report to the Guidance Office. Marnie Fitzpatrick, to the Guidance Office, please. Thank you!* another voice came over the loud speaker.

Whatever Marnie had to say to Brynne would have to wait for Round Two. She tossed Brynne a dirty look as she picked up her things. As Marnie walked to the door, she had to edge by her opponent, Jeremy Atwood, who was blocking the entrance to homeroom with his big forehead and his gigantic three-ring binder.

"Excuse you," Jeremy barked as Marnie tried to move around him.

"Yeah, yeah, yeah," she muttered and looked right past Jeremy.

Once she was in the clear, Marnie double-timed it down the hallway, up the stairs, through another corridor, and then into the main atrium, where Poughkeepsie Central's administrative offices were located. The Guidance Office was located in a small cluster of rooms, decorated with framed pictures of sailboats and sunrises accompanied by inspirational and empower-ing words like *achieve* and *leadership*.

*Yikes, this room is hokier than Ned Flanders.*

Marnie sat down on one of the worn-in, yet comfort-able couches in the common area and eyed the college brochures and outdated health pamphlets that were strewn about on the coffee table. She was just about to open one with the title, "If it feels good, then it's *real bad*," when her guidance counselor, Mrs. Robertson, popped her head out from behind her cubicle door.

"Hey, Marnie, nice to see you," she said warmly.

Marnie *adored* Mrs. Robertson, mostly because she didn't seem like an authority figure. She was more like a favorite older cousin who wanted everyone to learn from all the mistakes she'd made. Mrs. Robertson had a short cropped hairdo that stopped just above her pointy chin and she always wore dangling earrings. Today she had on silver hoops that had blue stones hanging within them. Marnie smiled when she thought about how the earrings would rate on Lizette's fierce-o-meter.

"Come in, come in." Mrs. Robertson waved Marnie over to her desk. "Just pretend you don't notice the mess."

Marnie wandered over to one of the chairs facing Mrs. Robertson and sat down.

"So I have good news," Mrs. Robertson said happily.

Marnie's ears perked up. "Really?"

Mrs. Robertson put on a pair of wire-rimmed glasses and peered at a folder on top of her desk. "Yes, I do. The class transfer you asked for last week went through! Isn't that great?"

Marnie furrowed her brow. "Class transfer?"

"Don't act like you don't remember. You came in here *begging* me to get you one class with that friend of yours. Nola James, right?"

In less frantic times, Marnie would have remembered that, no problem. But with the chaos of the last few days fresh in her mind, she could barely remember her middle name (which was Kathleen, after her grandmother).

"Right," Marnie sighed.

"Well, consider your wish granted, my dear. I was able to switch your morning study hall with your afternoon English class, so now you report to Mr. Quinn in room 108 during fourth period, just like Nola does."

Mrs. Robertson stamped the paper in a very official manner, which propelled Marnie's pulse into another stratosphere.

*I can't be in a class with Nola!*

She had to get out of this. Absolutely *had to*.

"I appreciate your help, Mrs. Robertson," Marnie

said, wringing her hands. "But my schedule is fine the way it is."

Mrs. Robertson reclined in her chair and raised her eyebrows curiously. "I'm sorry, hon. I can't switch it back."

"But maybe you could —"

"Marnie, once I issue a transfer, it's a done deal. I'm very sorry." Mrs. Robertson handed the paper to Marnie as the first-period bell rang. "You better get to class."

When Marnie stood up from her chair, the strain in her shoulder felt more like an open wound, a wound that Mrs. Robertson had poured twenty-six ounces of Epsom salts on. How could she spend the rest of the year sitting only a few feet away from her ex-best friend?

In a few hours, Marnie was going to find out.

# Chapter 4

As Mr. Quinn scribbled out the major themes in John Knowles's *A Separate Peace* on the dry-erase board, Nola kept her head down and her eyes focused on the doodles in her notebook, which she was drawing with Matt's KISS pencil.

She had spent the last few days reading this novel about the demise of a friendship and had only four more chapters left to go. But Nola had been unable to finish the book after her brawl with Marnie — reading it was much too painful. Now Mr. Quinn's lecture had turned to the theme of jealousy and Nola tried not to let any of his monologue sink in.

However, no matter how many squiggly lines or stick figures she drew, Nola couldn't help but hear Mr. Quinn say "envy" over and over again. Nola hadn't entertained the notion that her face-off with Marnie might have been rooted in envy, but at this moment, she wasn't as sure. Maybe she did fly off the handle because she was jealous of Marnie's growing friendship with Lizette. Maybe she was resentful that Marnie was meeting new people. But even if both those theories were true, did it excuse Marnie from giving something as sacred as her handmade birthday present to Lizette or blowing Nola off all the time?

The door to the room creaked open, and everyone turned in the direction of the sound. There stood Marnie, looking very willful and composed in a frilly skirt and knee-high boots. Nola's fingers locked up in a massive cramp the second she saw her.

"Sorry I'm late, Mr. Quinn," Marnie said cheerfully. She walked across the classroom and handed him a pink sheet of paper. "Mrs. Robertson switched my schedule, so I'll be in your class from now on."

Suddenly, Nola felt as though someone had body-slammed her. *Marnie is going to be in this class for the rest of the year? Does the universe hate me?*

"Yes, she did mention that," Mr. Quinn said as he held the paper up and inspected it carefully. "Take whatever seat you'd like, Marnie."

Nola quickly peeked over her right and left shoulders to see where the vacant desks were located. Much to Nola's horror, there were only two, and both of them were on a close diagonal from her spot. Either way, Marnie was going to be sitting near enough that Nola could reach out and yank Marnie's hair (which she was fighting the urge to do).

Nola watched Marnie as she contemplated her

options. She waited for the inevitable awkward eye contact, but it didn't come. Marnie passed by and sat in the desk that was diagonally in front of Nola and to the left, without any acknowledgment of Nola's presence.

Marnie's harsh dismissal angered Nola to the core. How could Marnie just pretend that Nola *wasn't even there*? Nola had expected a mean sneer or a "what*ever*" eye roll, but ignoring her altogether was beyond brutal.

Mr. Quinn repositioned himself near the dry-erase board. "Marnie, we're discussing *A Separate Peace*. Have you read it?"

"Yes, we just finished the book yesterday in Ms. Gresko's class," Marnie chirped.

Nola didn't have to see Marnie's face to know that she was batting her eyelashes and smiling. The girl had only been in the room for less than two minutes and she was already kissing up to the teacher.

*What a brownnoser.*

"Great! Right now we're talking about the role of envy in the story. Do you have anything to add to our discussion?" he asked.

Nola squirmed in her chair as she waited to hear Marnie's response.

"Actually, I do," Marnie replied, straightening her sweater. "I think Gene's jealousy of Finny is what really tore their friendship apart. If he had just *chilled out* and tried to be less of an *outsider*, then everything would have been fine."

Nola's mouth grew slack. *Oh, no, she didn't!*

"Well, that's one way to look at it." Mr. Quinn adjusted his red striped tie. "Anyone else have an opinion?"

Without thinking, Nola shot her hand up and waved it frantically, as if she were hailing a cab.

Mr. Quinn pointed at her. "Yes, Nola."

She gripped the top of her desk and swallowed hard. "Finny wasn't considerate of Gene's feelings *at all*. He was so busy being *self-obsessed* that he didn't even notice how much Gene was *hurting!*" Nola snapped.

Marnie's head whipped around, her eyes shooting daggers. But Nola just raised her eyebrows at Marnie and smirked impishly.

"You've got a point there, Nola. It isn't always easy to sympathize with Finny," Mr. Quinn said. He went to the dry-erase board and wrote: *Finny = Self-absorbed*

Marnie spun back to the front of the classroom and slouched over her desk in defeat.

Nola leaned back in her chair and grinned. She couldn't believe what she just did! Nola *never* volunteered to talk in class, let alone verbally spar with someone who had screwed her over big-time.

Nola had never felt good at Marnie's expense before but she couldn't help but feel that way now. In fact, she didn't just feel good — Nola felt victorious, like she'd won a small battle in the Fitzpatrick-James cold war.

The only thing Nola didn't realize just then was that she couldn't possibly win them all.

# Chapter 5

Marnie was absolutely furious after she left Mr. Quinn's class. She kept hearing Nola's voice echoing in her ears. *Self-obsessed? Not considerate of her feelings?* How dare Nola say those things?! Marnie had been a loyal, supportive friend to Nola, and for her to fixate on a couple of awkward weeks instead of remembering all the wonderful times they'd shared over the past *eight years* was just unconscionable. And to think, Marnie would have to endure Nola's taunts for two hundred or more school days. . . .

*If we were still talking to each other, I would DESTROY HER!*

Just as Marnie was storming down the crowded corridor, she felt someone grab her from behind by the waist. She nearly shrieked before a hand covered her mouth and she was pulled into a darkened classroom. Marnie was shaking with fear when whoever kidnapped her spun her around and grinned mischievously.

Then Marnie recognized a familiar pair of glinting eyes.

"Dane! You scared the crap out of me," she said, taking a few brisk steps away from him.

Dane flipped on the light switch and smiled widely.

"I saw you as I was leaving the A/V room and I couldn't help myself."

Dane looked so incredible that Marnie had to force herself to blink. He was wearing greenish khaki pants and a light blue button-down shirt with the sleeves rolled up. Marnie wished he would grab her again and kiss her, but he just stood still, gazing at her.

"What?" Marnie said, feeling self-conscious.

"Sorry. You're just so, *so* pretty." He shook his head as if he were waking himself up from a daydream.

Marnie's cheeks flushed pink. "I am?"

Dane chuckled. "How about we play a game?"

"What kind of game?" Marnie asked, hoping that no one would walk into this classroom and interrupt them.

"Well, every step you take toward me," Dane said as he locked his hands behind his back, "I have to give you a reason why you're pretty."

Suddenly, it was as if Marnie Fitzpatrick had never even heard of Nola James.

She grinned. "That's it?"

Dane nodded and moved his hands to his pockets. "Ready?"

She glanced at the clock in the science lab they were loitering in, and when the bell sounded, she swallowed hard. "Dane, I'm going to be late." Marnie hated sounding like a priss, but her Social Studies teacher Mr.

Zolnowski loved to write people up for tardiness, or any other noun with a "ness" attached to the end of it.

"I'm sure I can find a way to score you a pass," Dane said gallantly. "So are you in or out, Marnie?"

Marnie smiled, said nothing, and took one step forward.

"You have the most *amazing* green eyes," Dane said sweetly.

Marnie's heart fluttered as she took another step.

"I *love* the way you dress," he crooned.

Marnie glanced down at herself and gave another smile. She did look kind of hot today — she was wearing her favorite black knee-high boots, a Free People wildflower print skirt, and a cute ivory cap-sleeve sweater from Banana Republic. It was an innocent and flirty outfit with just a hint of biker-chic. Lizette had given her a few fashion tips recently, which Marnie thought improved her sense of style by 1,000 percent.

When she took another step toward Dane, he said, "Your smile is unbelievably gorgeous."

One more step and Marnie would be inches away from Dane and his strong arms. She could feel her body quivering as she put one foot in front of the other. She could feel Dane's hands reach out and grip her waist. She could feel him leaning down a bit, so that the right side of his cheek was barely touching hers.

"And your lips are delicious," he whispered.

Right now, Marnie didn't care if Mr. Zolnowski wrote her up for skanky-ness. She had to kiss Dane right now or else she was going to burst into scorching flames. But before she made even one move, Marnie reached over and flicked the light switch off.

"Nice," Dane murmured as he moved his hands up her back. Then she felt his palms cup her face, his thumb tracing the outline of her lips. She stood up on her tiptoes, and in seconds his mouth was on hers, his heart beating in the same accelerated rhythm as her own.

Marnie tried to think of words to describe how she felt just then, but the word *nice* wasn't even in the top ten on her list.

# Chapter 6

An hour later, Nola sat in the cafeteria, watching Matt and Evan Sanders inhale their bacon double cheeseburgers. Iris had a dentist appointment and hadn't come back to school yet, so Nola had to eat her fried fish sandwich within the confines of Guy-topia.

Usually, Nola would be uncomfortable in a situation like this one. Here she was, chowing down with two boys and being expected to get involved in a conversation that would probably contain topics such as "hard drive space," "Intel processors," and "RAM-osity" (a term that Matt had made up a few minutes ago). But Nola was still high off of the can of whoop-ass she opened on Marnie during English, so she felt as though she could do just about anything, including flirt with a perfectly tousled and adorable Matt.

Nola adjusted her thin yellow Benetton V-neck sweater a little so that it wasn't bunched up around her stomach and put her hair back in a low ponytail. Then she smiled and listened for a good segue.

"I don't get it." Evan wiped a ketchup blob off the corner of his mouth with a napkin. "How can you say that Pro Tools sucks?"

Matt took a swig of his Sunkist. "It only sucks if you

have to pay money for the program. You can download the free version and have a lot of the same functionality."

"Yeah, but you don't get as many effects and formatting options, right?" Evan asked.

"It's rock 'n' roll, man," Matt said, drumming his hands on the table. "You gotta keep it pure."

Then again, maybe Nola could just sit there and nod her head. That seemed like a good plan, too.

"What do you think, Nola?" Matt punched her playfully in the arm.

Every time he touched her, Nola felt as though her heart might tear at the seams.

"Um, I don't know," she said, hoping he'd accept that as an answer and move on to some other subject she didn't fully understand.

"Okay, let's look at it this way. Evan comes up to you and says, 'Hey, here's this program that costs a bunch of loot, and it will allow you to become louder, faster, and more versatile than any musician around.' But then I remind you that you already have a program which doesn't cost you a dime and gives you everything you already want," Matt said with a wink.

Nola's grin stretched across her face for miles. Matt wasn't just talking about music recording programs — he was trying to make her feel better about what had happened with Marnie.

*Could he be more fantastic?*

"I'm a sentimental girl," Nola said, her face flushing. "So no upgrading for me."

"That's right! In your face, Ev!" Matt rejoiced and high-fived Nola with over-the-top enthusiasm.

"You guys are nuts," Evan said, shaking his head.

"Yeah, well, we do it just to annoy you." Matt gave Evan a noogie, which Evan did not appreciate in the least.

"God, how did you manage to score a girlfriend? You are *so* juvenile sometimes," Evan said as he tried to smooth out his hair.

"Riley digs my rakish charm," Matt said.

Nola felt a piece of fish lodge in her throat, and coughed. *Riley. Girlfriend.*

"Rakish? Is the geek speaking in tongues now?" a voice boomed from behind.

Iris fell in next to Nola and tossed a large pint of Chinese food onto the table.

"Well, hello, Iris. Nice to see you, too," Matt said, grabbing the chopsticks before Iris could.

"I am in *no mood* for your shtick," Iris barked.

Matt could see she meant business so he handed them back over.

"What's wrong?" Nola asked.

"I have to get *braces!*" Iris whined. "Can you believe

that? How am I going to debate with a mouth full of metal?"

Evan looked as if he was about to say something sarcastic, but Iris stared him down until he decided to take another bite of his burger instead.

"I'm sure you'll do fine," Matt said sincerely. "And once they're off you'll be happy you had them. That's what Riley told me anyway."

Nola stuffed the remainder of her sandwich into her mouth and chewed hard. *Riley* again? *Damn, this is torture.*

Iris opened her container of pork fried rice, and steam rose into the air. "Really? Riley said that?"

Matt smiled. "Yeah, she did. In fact, you can talk to her about it next weekend. She's coming up for a visit."

Nola practically sprang up from her seat. *Riley?! Here?! With Matt? In his* house? *Near his bed? Oh. My. Freaking. God!*

"Cool, I will," Iris said softly as she picked at her food. "Thanks, Matt."

*This can't be happening.*

"Iris, I'm going to get an ice cream. Want something?" Evan inquired.

Iris perked up a bit. "Yeah, I'll come with you actually."

Once Evan and Iris left the table, Matt wasted no time in bringing up an awkward topic.

"So have you given any thought to my indecent proposal?" Matt nudged her with his elbow.

*Again with the touching! Why does he even do that if he doesn't* like *me?*

"I'm not sure," she said simply.

The fact was this: There was absolutely no way Nola could disregard the happy expression on Matt's face, or how bad she felt, every time he said Riley's name. How could she possibly bestow him with temporary best friend rights under these kinds of circumstances? It would drive her *insane.*

"Okay, how do you feel about a trial run? It'll be kind of like a *three*-day money-back guarantee. Only you can't send me back for a full refund."

Nola laughed. She was using every cell in her body to resist Matt's so-called rakish charm. But the thing was, Nola knew she didn't *have* to give in — she wanted to.

"Fine, we'll see how things go on a day-to-day basis," Nola replied, reminding herself to keep her feelings for Matt in check.

"Awesome. You won't regret it," Matt said as he stood up. He kissed her on the top of her head before sprinting off to the vending machine.

That tiny, innocent little kiss might as well have been a wrecking ball named "regret-osity," because when it hit Nola, all of her newfound confidence shattered to pieces.

Tuesday, September 18, 9:45 P.M.

**queenzee:** *hi* ☺

**marniebird:** *hey, how r u?*

**queenzee:** *awesome! just got back from watching s. lee do his thang at the skate park*

**marniebird:** *sweet! is he good?*

**queenzee:** *omg, marn. he's like, the poo, know what i mean?*

**marniebird:** *totally!*

**queenzee:** *r u doing anything fun?*

**marniebird:** *no, my nite has been v. blah*

**queenzee:** *whazzup?*

**marniebird:** *trying 2 come up with a campaign slogan*

**queenzee:** *care 2 share?*

**marniebird:** *don't laugh, ok?*

**queenzee:** *i won't*

**marniebird:** *No Marnie, mo problems! Vote Fitzpatrick for Treasurer!*

**queenzee:** *HAHAHAHAHAHA*

**marniebird:** *what?!*

**queenzee:** *does diddy know u r a gangsta?*

**marniebird:** *whatev, can u think of something better?*

**queenzee:** *um, yeah, with my eyes closed and my hands tied behind my back*

**marniebird:** *i guess that's y ur my manager, huh?*

**queenzee:** *right, u should leave this 2 me. u won't b sorry*
**marniebird:** *if u say so*
**queenzee:** *i say so. i also say we get brynne & grier 2 join the cause. maybe we can make posters, etc. at my house 2morrow nite?*
**marniebird:** *i dunno. brynne doesn't seem to like me*
**queenzee:** *what r u talking about? she likes u*
**marniebird:** *really? then why does she act like she's mad at me all the time?*
**queenzee:** *oh, that's just the way she rolls*
**marniebird:** *the way she rolls?*
**queenzee:** *i'm, like, speaking your language, gangsta*
**marniebird:** ☺
**queenzee:** *listen, brynne is always PMSing. just ignore her, ok?*
**marniebird:** *ok*
**queenzee:** *ugh, my dad's at my door, wants me to proofread something*
**marniebird:** *how cute!*
**queenzee:** *yeah, right. ttyl?*
**marniebird:** *l8ter*

# Chapter 7

Marnie never thought there would be a more magnificent sight than Lizette Levin's summer sprawl on Morgan Lake. But that had been before Wednesday night, when she set foot on the steps of Lizette's white-pillared house on Morgan Court.

Not only was it twice as big as the Levins' vacation spot, but it made Nola James's gigantic Victorian home on Winding Way seem like a dinky shack. The entire front yard was impeccably landscaped, and the hedges that circled around the property line were all trimmed to perfection. Even the flower beds, which should have been wilted by this point of the autumn season, were flourishing somehow.

Just the sight of the place helped Marnie push thoughts of seeing Nola's smug face in English class every day (*blech!*) to the back of her mind.

Marnie smiled as she rang the doorbell and waited for Lizette to answer. She pulled her Tarte Pucker Up lip balm out of the pocket of her vintage jean jacket and smeared some on her lips. The air was getting crisper every day, and Marnie was taking every possible measure to prevent chapping.

When the door flew open, Marnie opened her arms

wide, expecting to give her friend a hug. However, Marnie's hands quickly moved to her hips the moment she was met with the beady little eyes and sinister gap-toothed grin of Brynne Callaway.

"Oh, it's *you*," Brynne said sourly as she looked Marnie up and down.

"Who else would it be?" Marnie asked.

*Remember, Lizette said to ignore her.*

"The Thai food delivery guy," Brynne huffed. "Hope you already ate because there *won't* be any extras."

*Yeah, but how can you ignore a flesh-eating parasite?*

Marnie clenched her fists. It was bad enough that she had to spend forty-five minutes a day exchanging nasty looks with her ex-best friend. She certainly didn't need to take any of Brynne's cattiness.

Marnie was about to forcefully remove whatever was shoved up Brynne's butt when Grier Hopkins's sunny face popped up from behind Brynne's bony shoulders. Grier's pumpkin-colored hair was in a neat French braid. She looked so precious, Marnie wanted to put Grier in her pocket.

"Hello-hello!" Grier wriggled by a steadfast Brynne and gave Marnie a warm embrace.

"Sorry I'm late. My mom's open house ran a little long," Marnie said, inhaling the sweet scent of Grier's CK One perfume.

"You should see all the stuff Zee did!" Grier grabbed Marnie's hand and led her into the house while Brynne pouted and marched behind them.

Marnie nearly gasped when she entered the sunken living room with a stone-faced fireplace and wide-screen wall-mounted plasma TV. Lizette was knee-deep in Magic Markers and poster board, pointing the remote straight ahead and turning up the volume to her favorite 30 Seconds to Mars video. She was wearing a zip-up sweatshirt with the sleeves cut off and a drawstring purple velour mini. When she saw that Marnie had arrived, her eyes lit up.

"It about time you got here!" Lizette exclaimed. She waved Marnie over to the center of the room, where supplies were scattered left and right. There was a long, enormous sign with Marnie's name written in large bubble letters and the slogan — VOTE FOR THE MAJORITY LEADER OF THE FUN PARTY! — scrawled beneath it.

Marnie plopped down on the floor and stared in awe at Lizette's handiwork. "Wow, you *did* come up with something better!"

"You mean, something that will bounce Jeremy Atwood out of the race, right?" Lizette asked with a smug grin.

"Exactly," Marnie said, smiling.

The doorbell rang once again and everyone turned toward the hallway, where Brynne was still standing with her arms crossed firmly in front of her chest.

"The eats are here," Grier said, grinning.

Lizette jutted her chin out in Brynne's direction. "Hey, could you get that?"

"Why do *I* always have to answer the door?" Brynne barked.

Lizette shot her a stern look. "God, Brynne, could you *be* any more of a killjoy?"

Brynne sighed heavily and stomped away. A minute later, she charged into the living room with a huge paper bag and slammed it down on the rectangular oak coffee table (which Marnie recognized from the cover of last month's *Domino*). The spicy smell of curry wafted through the air, and Marnie licked her lips. She hadn't had dinner yet and once Grier began handing out containers of pad thai and udon noodles, her mouth started watering.

Lizette reached for a quart of pineapple chicken and coconut rice. She spooned some onto a paper plate and handed it to Marnie with a smile.

"Um, I don't remember ordering for *four* people," Brynne said with a heap of attitude as she broke apart a pair of chopsticks.

Marnie swallowed hard and brought her shoulders

back. Regardless of Brynne's obvious chemical imbalance, she couldn't allow the girl to push her around like this. "Oh, I'm sorry, Brynne. I completely forgot that you have the appetite of a *truck driver*."

"I do not!" Brynne sneered at Marnie and pushed her plate full of tandoori beef off to the side.

"Brynne *totally* got stung!" Lizette said, laughing so much that she needed Marnie to prop her up.

Marnie couldn't help but chuckle, too, especially when she glanced at Grier, whose face was crimson from trying not to laugh. Marnie felt newly empowered.

Once everyone composed themselves, they dug into their aromatic meals. Marnie only had one bite before she heard her phone beep. She leaned back and stretched a little until she could reach her tote bag, then nabbed her cell and sat back up. Marnie flipped it open and saw she had a message from Dane. Her breath immediately quickened, and she put her hand on her chest for a second to relax herself.

MISS ME YET?

"So what does the boyfriend have to say for himself?" Lizette asked as she chewed on a piece of garlic naan.

*Boyfriend?* Marnie thought. She and Dane had made

out a few times, but did that really mean he was her *boyfriend*? In middle school, kissing someone was staking claim on them, but were the same rules in effect now that she was a freshman? Marnie didn't have the slightest clue.

"How did you know it was Dane?" she asked.

Lizette nearly spit out her bread. "Puh-lease. You almost choked when you read the text message. Who else could it be from? Your *mom*?"

"C'mon, I'm not *that* bad," Marnie replied bashfully.

Grier picked at some tofu korma. "You must *really* like him."

Marnie tried not to lose her cool, but it was difficult to remain calm when an extremely sexy guy had just asked her, "Miss me yet?" In fact, Marnie was happy that she got the message while she was hanging out at Lizette's. Otherwise, Marnie would have already texted back, "Do I ever," instead of letting him wonder what she might be thinking. That was exactly the kind of mind game Marnie's sister, Erin, would have encouraged her to play.

"Oh, I have a great idea!" Lizette said after finishing off her Diet Coke. "Why don't you and Dane hang out with Sawyer and me on Friday?"

Even though she wasn't invited, Grier nodded her

head in approval. "I hear that new Italian restaurant that opened near Vassar is amazing."

Marnie was a tad squeamish about the prospect of hanging out with her kinda-sorta boyfriend and her current number-two crush *at the same time*. That had to be going against some sort of universal dating code, didn't it? And if not, was it okay to have an ambiguous relationship *and* a crush list, too? Regardless of the ethical concern, Marnie couldn't ignore how thrilled Lizette seemed to be at the prospect of double-dating, so Marnie hit the SNOOZE button on her freak-out-alarm and grinned widely.

"Okay, let me ask Dane." She tapped a quick text message into her phone — WANT 2 DBLE W LL & SL ON FRI?

Lizette popped up from the floor in excitement. "I'm gonna run upstairs and call Sawyer. Be right back."

As soon as Lizette left the room, Brynne tore her napkin into shreds and sprinkled it on top of Marnie's food. "I'm so outta here," she growled, and then stood so she loomed over Marnie and Grier like a dark shadow.

"But we're not finished with Marnie's posters yet," Grier said.

"Like I care," Brynne spat out. Then she pointed angrily at Marnie. "God, do you *sleep* in that jacket or something?"

Marnie shook her head in confusion as Brynne

stormed out of the house. "Why is she so pissed off at me?" she asked Grier.

"Well, Brynne and Zee used to be best friends, until . . ." Grier's voice trailed off.

"Until what?"

Grier made a strange face and shrugged her shoulders.

But as Marnie searched Grier's expression, she knew exactly what Grier meant. Brynne and Lizette had been just like Nola and Marnie. They'd told each other their secrets and never went more than a few hours without talking to each other. Then some new person came along and interfered with their perfect arrangement. Brynne was Lizette's Nola, and she was furious because she wasn't Lizette's priority anymore: Marnie was.

This whole situation was ridiculously unfair. All Marnie wanted to do was make friends with someone new. Why was everyone getting so mad at her for it?

Marnie snapped to attention when her phone beeped. She checked her in-box and saw that Dane had texted her back:

I'LL ANSWER UR QUESTION IF U ANSWER MINE

Marnie slapped her forehead. How could she have forgotten to respond to his first message?

She frantically typed on her keypad and sent him some pink Razr reassurance:

NEXT TIME I SEE U, U'LL KNOW HOW MUCH I MISS U

Within seconds, the phone was beeping in her hand.

:-) WE'RE ON 4 FRI. XO

Marnie sighed. Fortunately, there was *one* person who wasn't mad at her, one person who was extraordinarily, irrefutably hot.

And possibly her boyfriend . . .

# Chapter 8

Nola was in her room on Tuesday night, sitting at her computer and trying to do research for a global studies project. But all she could think about was how Matt had gone down the Marnie Fitzpatrick route in less than forty-eight hours.

On Monday, he'd told her that they'd go apple picking in the afternoon, which she'd been really excited about — Nola loved Golden Delicious apples in the fall. But when she'd met Matt in the high school parking lot after school, he backed out because "something came up" with his dad. (It was a lame excuse, but Nola hadn't called Matt on it, mostly because he looked too damn hot in his worn-in jeans and forest green crewneck sweater with a tiny tear in the right armpit.)

She'd also sent Matt a HOW R U? text message at around 4:30 P.M. It was now 8 P.M. and there hadn't been a response. The only thing left for Matt to do was take something special of Nola's and give it to someone else. Then the experience would be a prime example of déjà vu.

Nola's eyes filled with tears. She felt utterly stupid for thinking not only that Matt would be able to take Marnie's place (dumb), but that if he spent some more time with Nola, he'd suddenly realize that he was meant to be her love slave (even dumber).

Nola glanced at the clock on her nightstand and saw the minute hand move another millimeter. She knew deep down that he wasn't going to reply to her text message and that if there had been something wrong with his dad, he wouldn't have confided in Nola — he'd have most likely poured his heart out to his girlfriend, Riley Finnegan.

For a moment, Nola pictured what Riley might look like — her eyes, her hair, her chin, her smile. Riley Finnegan was definitely an Irish name, so there was a good chance that she had long wavy red locks that glistened in the sunlight, or eyes the color of shamrocks. Just imagining this girl holding Matt's hand or wrapping her arms around him gave Nola such intense chills that she grabbed a fleece throw off the edge of her bed and wrapped it around her shoulders tightly.

When she sat back down at her desk, Nola shook her head and tried to concentrate on her work. She had until Friday to write a short paper on Gandhi and still needed information on the partition of India. She'd done about ten different Google searches, which had provided her with a lot of material, but there were a few more gaps she had to fill in.

She straightened up in her chair and sipped some

water out of a plastic tumbler, then typed "India + Gandhi + sedition" into the text box. Nola stared at the words as the cursor blinked, and before she could contemplate what she was doing, she deleted everything and typed in "Riley Finnegan." Nola took a deep breath and clicked the SEARCH button.

Two pages of links jumped up on the screen, but Nola's attention went directly to the one in the middle —

www.myspace.com/rileyfinneganswake. She immediately went to click on the link, but then drew her hand back just as quickly.

*I can't do this,* she thought. *It'll make things worse.*

Suddenly, Nola heard a knock at her bedroom door, so she reduced the window on her screen.

"Come in."

The door popped open a few inches and her father poked his head in. "Working hard?" Mr. James had a habit of stating the obvious, but Nola adored this trait of his, even if it was borderline annoying.

"As usual. What's up?"

"Nothing. Your mom and I were just deciding where to send you to boarding school. We tossed a coin, so Greenland it is!" Her dad put both arms in the air as if he'd just won the Most Brilliant Sarcastic Comment Ever Award.

Nola laughed. "Good one, Dad."

Her father chuckled and walked into her room, but he stayed a safe distance away. Nola's dad was the king of personal space. Not that he was a cold person — he just wasn't the most affectionate guy around.

"Did you need something?" she asked.

"Yes, actually. Your mom and I wanted to let you know that we're having a family meeting tomorrow night." Her dad picked up the copy of *A Separate Peace* from her dresser and began flipping through it.

Nola's heart lodged in her throat. *Family meeting?* Every kid in America knew this was code for "awkward discussion about some uncomfortable subject and/or a choice we, your parents, just made that will change your life irrevocably and make you wish that someone would smother you while you sleep."

Then again, Nola had already suffered the loss of her best friend and the crushing blow of finding out the guy she was head over heels for was, in fact, head over heels for some Irish goddess with shamrocks for eyes. Could her life possibly get any worse? Probably not.

"What's the meeting about?" she asked.

"We hired a new babysitter for the boys, so he's coming over to meet everyone," her dad said, closing the book and returning it to its place on Nola's dresser. "Isn't that great?"

*Just what I need. Another person to cause trouble.*

"Awesome," she replied meekly.

Nola's dad nodded and made his way to the door, but then paused and turned back around. "Nola, is everything okay with you?"

*Oh, no.*

Nola had spent the last couple of days locked in her room, wailing into her Tempur-Pedic pillow so that no one would hear her. It seemed like her dad had caught on that something was wrong. Still, Nola was in no way ready to tell her parents what had happened between her and Marnie.

"Yeah, everything is fine."

"You've just seemed a bit . . . *off* lately," her dad pressed. "Or are your mother and I just imagining things?"

"Really, I'm okay," Nola said assuredly.

Her father sensed that he'd bugged her enough and relented. "All right, I'll pop in again when I put the boys to bed." Then he left the room and shut the door behind him.

*That was close.*

Nola turned back to her computer and brought up the Google search window. Although she kept willing herself to close it and return to her Gandhi project, the link to Riley's MySpace page haunted her. Nola grabbed the mouse and clicked on the link, no matter how loud the voice inside her head screamed, "Stop, you deranged lunatic!"

As the page loaded, Nola could feel her skin getting irritated. She didn't bother glancing down at her arms, because she knew that they'd be covered in raised red blotches.

However, Nola forgot about her hives when she saw Riley Finnegan's picture flash in front of her eyes. It was just a thumbnail-size image, but to Nola, it seemed as enormous as a billboard on I-87. Riley was nothing like the vague sketch Nola had drawn in her mind minutes ago. She was much more beautiful than that, or any other girl in Dutchess County.

Nola studied the photo carefully. Riley didn't have typical Irish features at all. No red hair, no green eyes. Actually, if she had seen Riley walking down the streets of New York City, Nola probably would have reported a Rosario Dawson sighting via text message to Gawker Stalker. Riley had the same dark penetrating eyes, light brown skin, and thick black hair, which fell down past her shoulders, but she had less prominent cheekbones and smaller, thinner lips.

Nola swallowed hard as she enlarged the photo to full view. Now she could see Riley's perfect nose and how the arches of her eyebrows made her seem inquisitive and wise. Nola gazed at Riley's smile — her teeth were a bit crooked, but they were gleaming as if they'd been buffed and polished by an overzealous dentist. That killer smile combined with her exotic, mysterious, other-worldliness made Riley Finnegan so gorgeous that Nola couldn't blame any guy for falling madly in love with her.

Nola tossed her fleece throw onto the floor. Her forehead felt hot, and perspiration was dripping down the back of her neck. She was about to scroll down and read Riley's profile when she heard her mother call up to her from the living room. Something about a laundry mishap.

*Oh, joy.*

As Nola turned off the computer monitor, she closed her eyes and prayed that her father was serious about the boarding school in Greenland. If not, her life in Poughkeepsie was going to become more complicated.

And a *lot* more painful.

# Chapter 9

Marnie wasn't in the greatest of moods on Wednesday morning. Not only was she not able to wear her favorite burgundy textured tights to school (there was a huge hole in the knee), but Mr. Quinn decided to give his English class a vocabulary pop quiz, complete with true or false and multiple-choice questions.

Marnie tapped her pen on the edge of her desk as she tried to recall the definition of "omniscient." Did it mean "the quality of being everywhere present at the same time" or "knowing all things"? She had been waffling between these two answers for close to five minutes now and was unable to pick one over the other. Marnie hadn't been studying her vocab words as much as she should, but what was really preventing her from deciding was this intense feeling that she was being stared at.

Marnie whipped her head around quickly to confirm her suspicion and when she did, Nola quickly looked down at her paper and began scribbling.

*God, why is she being such a brat?*

For the past two days, Marnie had done her best to pretend Nola wasn't sitting a few feet away from her in English class. In fact, she was trying to put her friend-ship with Nola behind her and focus on the new people in her life, people who were laid-back and cool and not wound as tightly as her ex-best friend. However, it was quite obvious that Nola wasn't following the same plan, otherwise she wouldn't be agitating Marnie by glaring at the back of her head all the time.

"Class, you have five more minutes left," Mr. Quinn announced as he reclined in his desk chair with today's newspaper.

Marnie swallowed hard. She still had six questions to go. How was she going to focus with Nola's brain-waves mucking up her concentration? There was only one solution.

Marnie reached into the right pocket of her dark indigo, embellished Rock & Republic jeans and pulled out her Razr phone. She held it under the desk so Mr. Quinn couldn't see her and then typed a text message as she kept her eyes trained on her quiz paper. Marnie leaned back in her seat and glanced at the screen to make sure she didn't make any mistakes. PLS STOP STARING @ ME, the message said.

*Perfect, now I can get on with my quiz.*

Marnie scrolled through her address book quickly and hit the SEND button after she'd selected Nola's name. Then she put her phone back in her pocket and decided that "omniscient" meant "knowing all things."

Marnie hadn't even finished reading the next

question when she felt her Razr vibrating against her leg. She thought about ignoring it and zipping through the rest of her quiz, but instead she snuck another peek at her phone underneath her desk.

It was a reply from Nola.


U R AN EGOMANIAC. I WASN'T STARING.


Marnie snapped her phone shut with utter disdain. How could Nola have the audacity to deny it? Marnie had caught Nola staring at her at least a dozen times since Monday. Actually . . .

Marnie spun around in her seat and just like before, she caught Nola frantically snapping her head down at the last possible second.

*Gotcha!*

"Is something wrong, Marnie?" Mr. Quinn's voice sounded very perturbed.

Marnie slowly turned toward the front of the class-room and met Mr. Quinn's disapproving gaze.

"No, I'm fine," she said apprehensively.

Mr. Quinn leaned forward and pointed at Marnie with a red pen. "If you don't keep your eyes on your own paper, I'll have to give you a zero. Understand?"

A collective snicker echoed through the room.

Marnie could feel her cheeks getting hot and her palms were sticky all of a sudden.

"I understand," she whispered.

"Three more minutes," Mr. Quinn said before returning to the sports section.

Marnie tried to block Nola's stupid message out of her mind, but no matter how many times she looked at her quiz, the only thing Marnie could think of was the word *egomaniac*.

*There's no way I'm letting* her *get the last word.*

Marnie flipped open her phone again and typed out another text. Her nimble fingers were flying across the keypad while she checked out the large clock over the classroom door. The second hand was zipping along and beads of perspiration started to form on Marnie's forehead when she realized that she only had one minute to answer the remaining four questions. Still, nothing seemed more important at this moment than putting Nola in her place.

When Marnie finished writing, she peered down at her phone and reviewed her message: MY MISTAKE. U MUST B RETARDED THEN. She knew it was a tad harsh, but Marnie wasn't about to forget that Nola was the reason she'd been reprimanded in front of the entire class, or all the other instances when she was monumentally embarrassed because of something Nola had done. On top of that, Nola had the gall to call her an egomaniac, after all the attention *she* had heaped on Nola since grammar school! How insane was that?

Marnie hit the SEND button with the strong feeling that her actions were completely justified. In fact, she figured that Lizette would have done the exact same thing in this situation. No doubt about it.

"Thirty seconds left," Mr. Quinn said loudly so that everyone would hurry up and race to the quiz finish line.

Marnie didn't even bother reading the rest of the multiple-choice questions. She just circled the letter *C* for all of them. At least she had a 25 percent shot of getting it right. And if she got a low score, Marnie would just ace the next quiz, no problem.

The sound of the dismissal bell rang out and Marnie passed her paper to the front row, where Mr. Quinn collected them. She gathered her tote bag from the floor and held her English book in the crook of her left arm. Then Marnie felt that infuriating staring sensation again. Couldn't Nola take a meteor-size hint?

Marnie jerked her head to the side, hoping that she'd catch Nola off-guard and in mid-stare, but she wasn't at her desk. Marnie looked around the room and Nola was nowhere to be found. Then Marnie's cell phone vibrated once more. She dug into her pocket and pulled out her Razr so she could check out the message she was sure was from Nola.

KISS MY BUTT!

It was strange — two weeks ago, Marnie might have read a text like this and laughed, thinking it was a joke. But this was no laughing matter, which was why Marnie deleted Nola's messages and cell number from her phone.

# Chapter 10

When Nola entered the living room on Wednesday evening, she never expected to see her kid brothers, Dennis and Dylan, also known as the Terrible Twins, sitting on the navy blue Crate & Barrel couch, completely still and relaxed. (Maybe her mother had given them a small dose of Valium.) In between them sat a very stiff-looking young man, dressed in a pink button-down shirt, sweater vest, jeans, and black Pumas. The guy kind of resembled Christian Bale, but instead of giving off the brooding, "I'm Batman" vibe, he was radiating this obnoxious, "I know everything and I'm trying *real* hard to show it" vibe. Nola glanced at her parents, who were on opposite sides of the room, staring at the guy adoringly.

Nola didn't like the look of this one bit.

"Hey, honey. Come over here and sit down." Her mom patted the spot next to her on the adjacent love seat.

Nola shoved her hands in her pockets, walked over to the love seat, and sat down on the arm instead.

Her dad was standing near the fireplace, stroking his goatee as if he was thinking about the right way to tell Nola something like, "Honey, this is Mr. Peabody.

68

He's going to escort you to Greenland. Remember to dress warm, and that we love you. Don't forget to write!"

Nola steadied herself when her father cleared his throat and clapped his hands together, which meant he was ready to call this meeting to order.

"Okay, fellow Jameses," he said, upbeat and jovial as ever. "As you all know, your mother and I have been searching for a new babysitter to take Colleen's place."

Nola sighed at the thought of Colleen, a sweet, considerate Polish woman in her early thirties, who made a kick-ass batch of walnut-covered sticky buns and never told her parents that she served them as an afternoon snack. Colleen was around for a grand total of eight weeks, after which she snapped due to the twins' relentless torture.

"We interviewed a lot of candidates, but one applicant really exceeded our expectations," her mom said effusively.

Nola could only guess that the applicant in question was the guy sitting on the couch with his hands folded in his lap.

"So we'd like you to welcome Ian Capshaw into our home," her father continued. "He'll be here, looking after the boys every weekday between the hours of two thirty and eight o'clock."

Her mom touched Nola on the knee lovingly. "I'm going to do everything in my power to get home by then, sweetie."

As much as Nola wanted to believe her mom, she had a strong feeling that she'd be picking up the slack whenever her mother had to stay late at the hospital.

"Does anyone have questions?" her father asked.

Nola raised her eyebrows. *How much do you wanna bet Ian here doesn't last two weeks?*

Dennis slowly lifted his hand in the air.

Nola's dad pointed two finger guns in his son's direction. "Shoot, my boy."

Dennis turned toward Ian and gazed up at him. "How old are you?"

Ian didn't even crack a kid-friendly smile. "Seventeen," he said.

"He's a freshman at Vassar," Nola's mom added, turning to him. "What are you studying again?"

Ian scratched at his ear and then looked at Nola. He paused for a second, as if he'd forgotten what classes he'd enrolled in altogether, and then shook his head. "Uh, right now I'm taking two American culture classes —"

"American *culture*?" Nola cut in abruptly.

At first, she had no idea why she'd spoken up, but soon she realized that the subject sounded completely fake. Did the college offer courses on baseball because it was America's favorite pasttime? Was *The Simpsons and Philosophy: The D'oh of Homer* on the required reading list? Ian's weird hesitation just added to her suspicions. What if this Ian character was just some creep who was planning on taking advantage of the James family and fleecing them for all they were worth?

And there was something about his mannerisms — the cool stare, the narrowed eyes, the permanent scowl — that bothered her, too. Did her parents decide to hire him because he was stern and would be able to discipline the boys? Perhaps. Regardless, she had to find out more about Ian before she could begin to trust him.

"Don't you mean American *history* or something?" Nola added, crossing her arms.

"No, it's American *culture*," Ian said, visibly irked by the disbelief in Nola's voice.

"Never heard of it," she said, glaring.

Her father gave her a look of warning, which Nola ignored.

"I wouldn't expect a freshman in high school to know much about it," Ian replied in a condescending, superior tone that made the fine hairs on Nola's arms stand up.

*Oh, my god, this guy is even more of an egomaniac than Marnie!*

Her mom tried to defuse the growing tension in the room with some old-fashioned hospitality. "Ian, would you like some coffee?"

Ian nodded. "That would be nice, thank you."

Dr. James turned to Nola and smiled. "You know where we keep the biodegradable filters, don't you, dear?"

And with that, Nola had been banished to the kitchen, where she couldn't interrogate Ian the Giant Dorkwad any longer.

As Nola poured some fresh Colombian grounds into the coffeemaker, her father wandered in and got out a mug from the cupboard. It was one he'd brought back from a pharmaceutical conference in El Paso, Texas. He stood next to Nola for a moment before putting a hand on her shoulder and squeezing. Then he wandered over to the fridge and got a carton of milk.

"Give Ian a chance, Nola," he said. "He has strict orders to stay out of your way. Honest."

Nola smiled a little, knowing that there was probably a shred of validity to what her dad had said. "Okay, I'll lighten up."

"Good." He put the milk on the counter and started to head back into the living room. "Besides, you'll be so busy hanging out with Marnie, you won't even notice that he's around."

Nola almost collapsed once her dad left. She had to tell her parents about Marnie at some point — they'd know something was up when Marnie didn't show up for their traditional Friday night sleepover. Then again, Nola hadn't told her parents about lots of things, like Matt's offer to be her best friend by proxy, or that she was crazy about Matt even though he already had a girl-friend who looked as though she'd been crowned Miss Teen Universe — *several times*.

But Nola knew that last little tidbit wasn't something she would ever tell her parents. It was a secret that she'd only reveal to Marnie, the girl who she didn't even know, or like, anymore.

# Chapter 11

CAMPAIGN DOS AND DON'TS

- DO dress for success, but don't forget to add some MAD FLAVAH! That means NO wrap dress and NO Express. Zee suggests a look that's Chelsea Clinton (cute tailored navy blue blazer) meets Gwen Stefani (sizzling platform red patent leather shoes)
- DON'T engage in mud-slinging with Jeremy Atwood. It's not always classy to be brassy (Thanks, CosmoGIRL!)
- DO mention Erin as much as possible without giving myself the dry heaves (Paul Bunyan-size sigh)
- DON'T get caught making out with Dane in the listening library — a sex scandal could ruin everything!

On Thursday afternoon during the weekly student council meeting, Marnie leaned back in her seat and tapped her pencil on her desk. Tom Whitford, last year's junior-class president, was speaking to students about election protocol. In a few minutes, the kids who were running for office would have to stand up in front of the group and discuss their political platform.

For some reason, the usually well-prepared, write-everything-down-in-list-form Marnie was taken completely by surprise. Tom said he'd announced this at last week's meeting, but all she could remember was Lizette fending off Jeremy Atwood and nothing else. At the moment, Marnie was trying to put a mental list of pertinent information together, but she was coming up blank.

*Political platforms?* The only platforms Marnie could talk about with any kind of authority were the patent leather ones she had described in her Campaign Dos and Don'ts list. Marnie swallowed hard. How was she going to go head-to-head with Jeremy the Wonder Jerk without seeming like a total airhead?

Marnie glanced down at her watch. Any second now, she would be called up to the podium in lecture hall 4. Marnie lifted her head and began to look around the room. Almost every high-ranking Major was sitting in the audience, but Lizette and Dane were nowhere in sight. Marnie closed her eyes and wished for either one of them to come to her rescue.

"Okay, Marnie Fitzpatrick and Jeremy Atwood, you're up next," Tom bellowed.

Marnie stood and walked slowly to the podium. Out of the corner of her eye, she saw Jeremy taking large, brisk steps in the same direction. He looked just as self-righteous as he had when he'd insulted her last week. In fact, Jeremy was also wearing the exact same thing — an old brown pullover sweater that was pilling, a light wash pair of jeans, and white sneakers that belonged on either a tourist or a registered nurse. Didn't he have more outfits in rotation, or a good stylist? After all, he was in the public eye.

As Jeremy took his place by her side, Marnie concentrated on lengthening her spine the way Ms. Cirque du Soleil had shown her in yoga class the other day. She inhaled deeply and tried to center herself. But Marnie couldn't stop wondering why Lizette hadn't shown up to the meeting like she'd promised she would at lunch today. Was Lizette pissed at her about something?

*Not now*, Marnie chastised herself. *Chin up, chest out, shoulders back.*

Tom approached the microphone at the podium. "I'm going to open the floor for questions, and each candidate will have one minute to respond."

Marnie became a little nervous as she watched Jeremy push his sleeves up and crack his knuckles. Then he flashed her a pompous grin, as if he was thinking about how he was going to obliterate her. Marnie raised her eyebrows at him. Whatever anxiety she was feeling miraculously dissipated — she wasn't going to let arrogant, geeky Jeremy get the better of her. If Marnie had to B.S. her way through this mini-debate, so be it. Jeremy was just about to find out how quick Marnie was on her feet.

Sally Applebaum, curly-haired heiress to the Dutchess County comptroller's throne, cleared her throat and said, "I would like to know your position on class dues."

Jeremy nodded to Marnie as if to say, "Ladies first."

But Marnie took a step back as if to say, "You go ahead, *loser*."

Jeremy moved up and leaned into the microphone with bravado. "Personally, I think class dues are a necessary evil. Nobody likes coughing up twenty dollars a month, but without our contributions, we wouldn't be able to put together a phenomenal end-of-the-year trip, or the Spring Fling dance. So if I'm elected treasurer, I will continue enforcing class dues."

Marnie rolled her eyes as the group applauded and Jeremy smiled smugly. Still, as dorky as he was, Marnie knew it would be hard to counter that fairly reasonable and well-spoken answer. As she stood there, waiting for the moderator to instruct her, Marnie's baffled mind turned to Lizette again. Why would Lizette nominate her for treasurer, offer to be her campaign manager, and then bail on a vital student council meeting instead of cheering her on? Lizette had to be upset at Marnie — that was the only way to explain it. But why? What could she have done to set her off? Marnie quickly reviewed the last twenty-four hours in her head and couldn't come up with a thing.

And then she realized something: She never second-guessed herself like this when she was friends with Nola. Not once.

Marnie steadied herself behind the podium and took a deep breath. She was about to say whatever nonsense that was scrambling around in her brain. But the sound of the door squeaking open caught her attention. Marnie looked up and saw Dane standing in the back of the room, smirking deviously.

"Can I interrupt for a sec?" he asked in a loud, yet affable voice.

Of course, Dane being the amazing, popular, well-liked guy he was, no one had any objections.

Dane dashed over to the podium. "Sorry, guys. You can't hear anything in the back row. There must be something wrong with the microphone."

Marnie's brow furrowed. *What is he up to?*

Dane stood next to Marnie and began fiddling with the mic wire with his right hand. While everyone was distracted by Dane's technical acumen, he sneakily took Marnie's wrist in his left hand. She looked at him curiously when she felt him press a piece of paper into her palm — she knew the podium was blocking everyone's view, so he must have been giving her some secret message.

Dane winked when he let go and sprinted off to the back of the room. When Marnie opened her hand and quickly read the note, her cheeks flushed pink.

> *Can't double-date without a first date of our own.*
> *Meet me by my locker at 4:45.*
> *— Dane*
> *PS: Say that class dues are a form of economic*
> *oppression and you'd rather organize more fund-raisers.*

Marnie giggled every last ounce of nervousness away. Then she winked at Dane and leaned into the microphone with an "I *make* the rules" kind of confidence that a friend of hers would have described as fierce, had she'd been there like she'd promised.

"Yeeee-haw!" Dane cried out when his neon orange bowling ball sent ten pins toppling down one by one. He spun around and did a celebratory dance that was part shimmy and part do-si-do.

Marnie sat behind the score-keeping machine,

laughing out loud at the sight of him. After the student council meeting, she'd made a vow not to waste valuable date-with-Dane time worrying about anything, and that included whether or not she'd unwittingly angered Lizette.

"*Yeehaw?*" Marnie got up and pulled her jeans down by the belt loopholes so they sat ultra low at her hips. "No wonder you don't have any rhythm. You, good sir, are a hick."

Dane strolled over to Marnie and put his hands on her waist. His fingertips were right underneath her cardigan, caressing the lower part of her tummy. "Well, this hick has skills, the likes of which you have never seen."

Marnie slowly ran her hands up Dane's arms. She could feel how toned and contoured they were, even underneath his long-sleeved J. Crew polo shirt. Then Marnie placed her hands on the nape of his neck and stood on tiptoe so her nose grazed the corner of his lips. Dane kissed her lightly at first, then deeper. He tasted exactly like a peppermint candy cane, and if Marnie hadn't been standing in the middle of Hoe Bowl Mardi-Bob on a league bowling night, she would have kissed and kissed him until he dissolved.

Dane stepped back a little and Marnie put the heels of her red-and-tan rental shoes back down on the shiny waxed floor. He rested his chin on the top of her head and let out a satisfied sigh. "See what I mean?"

Marnie's head felt light, like it was made out of cotton. "I think it's my turn."

"Good luck," Dane said, and gave her a kiss on the forehead. "You're going to need it."

"Are you kidding? I'm just warming up," Marnie said as she sashayed over to the ball return and stuck her hands over the air dryer.

"I should hope so." Dane looked up at the scoreboard and smirked. "You've only knocked down *three* pins."

Marnie picked up her five-pound bright pink bowling ball and squinted at Dane. "Prepare to meet the Sphere . . . of *Death*."

Dane laughed so hard he nearly spit out his fountain soda. "What's that?"

Marnie was about to explain the whole sordid story behind this infamous phrase when she noticed the big lump in her throat. The "Sphere of Death" reference was one of the most sacred inside jokes Marnie and Nola had shared, and she was choking up at the thought of it, even though it was a really funny memory.

Marnie tried to get a grip and remind herself that she was here with *Dane Harris*! Her dream guy! She had made it through the past few days of seeing/ignoring/text-fighting with Nola in English class and she had managed not to shed a single tear. Now was definitely not the time to break down!

But when Marnie envisioned her and Nola spending their allowance on rubbery hot dogs at the snack bar and trying to win an enormous plush Elmo doll at the crane game, she became so overcome with emotion she could barely see straight. Deep down Marnie knew that if she and Nola were still friends, Nola would have been at today's student council meeting, making goofy faces, and yet supporting her all the way.

But before Marnie could snap herself out of this unexpected funk, she heard her name being called out multiple times, as if there were an echo.

"Marnie!"

"Marnie!"

She leaned to her right and saw Nola's brothers, Dennis and Dylan, running toward her at full throttle. Marnie knew them well enough to know that they were about to tackle her, so she jumped out of the way right when they were in leg-clipping range.

"No fair!" Dennis said with disappointment. "You moved."

Dylan just smiled and waved hello.

Marnie wasn't happy to see the boys, and she was even less happy when she realized that Nola could be lurking around the corner. But then a good-looking guy in a sweater vest and Pumas jogged toward her, and all of a sudden Marnie had difficulty remembering what she was worried about.

"Hey, sorry about that," the boy said, out of breath. "I just started babysitting these kids, and they're a bit unruly."

*Babysitting, huh? Lucky Nola.*

"Don't worry. I'm used to it," Marnie said.

He made a confused face. "You are?"

Marnie leaned down and looked Dennis and Dylan in the eyes. "If you guys don't behave, I will spend the rest of my life making you *pay*," she said through clenched teeth.

Within seconds, the twins quieted down and went to find their bowling balls without terrorizing anyone else.

"I can't believe it," the guy said, raising his eyebrows in astonishment. "How did you do that?"

But Marnie wasn't about to explain it, even if a cute, make that a *very* cute, stranger was curious. Besides, flirting with the babysitter while her kinda, sorta boyfriend was standing right there would be pretty rude, wouldn't it?

"I have special powers," Marnie said slyly.

*Wait, that's not flirting, right?*

The boy flashed Marnie a quick grin and then darted after Dennis and Dylan.

"What was that all about?" Dane asked as he followed the mystery guy with his eyes. "Do you know those kids?"

Marnie opened her mouth in an effort to explain but could feel herself choking up again.

*God, now I can't even talk about Nola's stupid brothers without getting all weepy? What is the matter with me?*

"Are you all right?" Dane asked with concern.

"Yeah, uh, I'm fine." Marnie wiped away a tear that managed to meander its way down her cheek.

Dane moved in and put his arm around Marnie. "You look upset. Maybe you should sit down."

"Actually, I'm going to run to the bathroom," Marnie said, sniffling.

Dane couldn't look more bewildered. "Oh, okay."

Marnie gave Dane a quick peck on the cheek and walked briskly toward the ladies' room. She tried to keep the door in her line of vision so she wouldn't see any more reminders of the fun times she and Nola had shared. Marnie tried to forget about how hard she'd laughed when Nola would bowl grandma-style or how Nola would squeal with embarrassment when Marnie danced around their lane on Disco Bowl nights. She could feel the tears building up and the tension rising in her chest.

When she pushed through the bathroom door and locked herself in a stall, Marnie was grateful to be home free.

Thursday, September 20, 7:11 P.M.

**mheatherly:** *hey, n*
**nolaj1994:** *hi*
**mheatherly:** *busy?*
**nolaj1994:** *not really*
**mheatherly:** *did u hear the big news?*
**nolaj1994:** *no. what?*
**mheatherly:** *really? wow, i thought u'd b the first to know that i turned into a jackass*
**nolaj1994:** *:-) stop, u r not*
**mheatherly:** *seriously nol, i'm sorry for flaking out on you the other day, and for being so unavailable*
**nolaj1994:** *it's ok*
**mheatherly:** *yeah, if by "ok" u mean "a real crappy thing to do to a friend"*
**nolaj1994:** *good, we're on the same page ;-)*
**mheatherly:** *atta girl*
**nolaj1994:** *is everything all right? u haven't been at school*
**nolaj1994:** *u still there?*
**mheatherly:** *just the usual bs, can we talk about it later?*
**nolaj1994:** *oh, sure*
**mheatherly:** *what i wanna know is, r u free tomorrow night?*
**nolaj1994:** *yes, but it's my first fri sleepover night post-marnie brawl. i won't b much fun*

**mheatherly:** *r u kidding? this is the perfect chance for me 2 impress u with my marnie impersonation!*

**nolaj1994:** *u r scaring me*

**mheatherly:** *come on, it'll be awesome. i'll do anything u and marnie used 2 do*

**nolaj1994:** *including each other's makeup?*

**mheatherly:** *well, almost anything*

**nolaj1994:** *LOL*

**mheatherly:** *is that a yes?*

**nolaj1994:** *fine, but u r NOT sleeping over!*

**mheatherly:** *aw, 2 bad I won't get 2 c u in ur pjs*

**nolaj1994:** *afraid not*

**mheatherly:** *we'll have a great time anyway. should i bring the movie?*

**nolaj1994:** *sure, but nothing . . . sketchy*

**mheatherly:** *HAHAHA, what u must think of me! :-)*

**mheatherly:** *c u in the a.m.*

**nolaj1994:** *u bet*

**mheatherly:** *g'night*

**nolaj1994:** *bye*

# Chapter 12

"*Step Up?*" Nola asked with astonishment when she opened the red Netflix envelope that Matt had handed to her before sitting down at the head of her bed.

She'd been expecting a movie with any one of the following: AK-47s, kung fu, drag racing, the mafia, strippers, headbangers, gangbangers, and explosions that brought down high-rise buildings. This was, in fact, the magical recipe for any film that would keep teenage boys sitting glued to the tube on a Friday night.

But a *chick flick*? Matt must have been smoking some questionable substances while he was out of school and tending to his mystifying "dad" problems.

"I thought the tagline was fitting," Matt answered with a crooked grin. He was wearing a zip-up sweatshirt with a skull on the front and a pair of loose corduroys that had threads hanging off of the cuffs. *Scrumptious*, Nola thought. "Look, I wrote it down on the envelope."

Nola flipped the envelope over and smiled when she read Matt's messy scrawl out loud. "Every second chance begins with a first step."

"Doesn't that bring tears to your eyes?" he said sarcastically.

"Wow, you really *are* a jackass," Nola joked.

Matt grabbed a pillow from behind his back and threw it at Nola. "Hey, I am offering to watch a movie with *dancing*. And horrible acting! Can't you see that I'm sorry for being a bad substitute best friend?"

Nola turned her back to Matt and headed over to the DVD player. She could see that he was sorry all right, but she didn't want him to see her eyes watering up. As much as she liked Matt — and boy, did she *like* Matt — Nola couldn't help but wish that the old, sweet Marnie was here, dressed in her lavender nightshirt and munching on homemade Chex Party Mix, ready to swap boy stories and embarrassing past moments and dreams of the future.

Nola wiped at her eyes with her palms and began chanting in her head: *Matt Heatherly is on your bed! Rejoice! RE-JOICE!*

But it didn't work. Friday night sleepovers with Marnie were like the laws of physics — indisputable. So far, nothing about this evening felt right. Nola thought for a moment that maybe she should just pass Marnie an apologetic note during one of their nasty Cameron Diaz–versus–Scarlett Johansson stare-downs in English class and take back what she'd said in their text-spat, just so she didn't have to go through the misery of missing her best friend.

But then Nola felt a pair of arms wrap around her from behind. A pair of hands clasped together in front of her. A cheek pressed up against her cheek. When the arms squeezed her gently, her breath escaped her lips like a whisper.

"You looked like you needed one of these," Matt said softly.

*Wait a minute . . . Is Matt holding me?*

Yep, he sure was. What did this mean? Nola felt a prickly sensation crawling up the back of her legs and her shoulders tensing up. What should she do if Matt spun her around and kissed her? Dodge him? Throw him down on the floor and devour him? Nola's thoughts were sprinting ahead of her, and she couldn't catch up.

The door flew open.

"Everything okay in here?"

It was Ian. Stupid, idiotic, vest-wearing Ian!

Matt broke away from Nola and shoved his hands in his pockets. "Yeah, we're just hanging out."

This didn't seem to fly with Ian, who was sneering at Matt as if the boy had clubbed a baby seal with his bass guitar. "Then why is the door closed?"

Nola's face turned as pink as the ostrich she'd hidden under the bed with all the other stuffed animals. Wasn't this pretentious college student being paid to watch her little brothers, *and* stay out of her way? God, he was so irritating, and she'd known him for less than twenty-four hours!

"I'm about to put in a movie. We don't want any outside noise coming in. It'll be hard to hear," she explained, flustered.

Ian stood there, glaring at the both of them as he clearly tried to think of something that would refute such reasonable and sound logic. "Well, leave it open a crack."

Matt tossed Ian a confused look. "Why?"

"Why *not?*" Ian asked. "Are you trying to hide something?"

Nola was so embarrassed she nearly sank to the floor. "Fine, we'll leave it open a little if you leave us alone. Okay?"

Ian put his hands on his hips and gave them a holier-than-thou head nod. "Good." Then he was gone in a flash the moment he heard Dylan scream, "*Ow*, Dennis! My nose is bleeding!"

Nola was almost afraid to look at Matt, but that fear subsided once she heard him laughing.

"Oh, my god, he totally thinks you and I are going to go at it!" he said, snickering.

Nola hid her face with her hands momentarily. "I know. What a *loser*," she mumbled.

Matt's laughter became even louder. "Come on, Nol. Don't be embarrassed. It's actually hilarious!"

*Then why did you put your arms around me a minute ago?!* an exasperated voice yelped in Nola's head. She'd never been more baffled by a guy — ever. One minute Matt acted sweet and affectionate, like he was interested in being more than a friend, and the next minute he was hysterically laughing at the idea of Nola and him "going at it."

Was she that hideous?

One thing was for sure: Friendship was a lot simpler when it involved just her and Marnie.

"Sorry, sorry. I'll calm down," Matt said while taking deep breaths.

"Maybe we should just start the movie." Nola began to set up the DVD player and tried to avoid looking at Matt.

"Wait, aren't we supposed to braid each other's hair first?"

Nola's face broke into a smile. Why did Matt have to be *so freaking cute* all the time?

A cell-phone beep sounded and Nola walked over to her desk, where her phone was charging.

Matt reached for his back pocket and pulled out his cell. "It's mine," he said, flipping it open. The corners of his mouth turned up into a grin. "Just a text from Riley," he said.

*Oh, great. Here we go.* Nola gnashed her teeth as Matt typed a message out on the keypad.

Within a few seconds, Matt's phone beeped again.

He chuckled when he read Riley's reply. "I told her that we were watching *Step Up* tonight and she's just tearing it apart. Now I'm even more excited to see it."

Nola's eyes grew wide. Matt told his girlfriend that he was spending his Friday night at *another girl's house* and this wasn't cause for jealousy? Maybe Nola *was* that hideous.

"She said you'd like the choreography, though," Matt continued as he kept toying with his cell phone. "Apparently it's kind of J. Lo meets Alvin Ailey."

Riley's MySpace profile immediately popped into Nola's brain. Nola had looked at the page a lot since Wednesday night and had taken another peek right before Matt came over this evening. She'd memorized practically every factoid about Matt's one-and-only, which was hard to do because the neon-colored page design was visually distracting.

*General interests: I likes me geetar and me blog (and talking like Popeye, obviously)*

*Music: Nina Simone, Iron & Wine, Damien Rice, Cat Power, Acid House Kings, Sunny Day Real Estate, Smothered in Argyle, Belle & Sebastian, Amos Lee, Creeper Lagoon, Elvis Costello, Men Without Hats, Mark Scudder, The Grifters, Junkrod Joe and the Cadillac Hearse, The Sea and Cake*

*Movies: One word — Borat.*

*TV: The Biggest Loser (Don't judge me!)*

*Books: Anything by David or Amy Sedaris — they were sent to Earth as prophets, so listen to them very carefully!*

*Heroes: a certain bass player/visionary concert promoter*

But what stood out the most had been the "About Me" section of Riley's MySpace page. It was only a sentence, but it had made a great impact on Nola because of how strong-willed and empowering it sounded.

*If you can't accept me at my worst, you don't deserve me at my best.*

Nola felt the same way now as she did when she'd first read those words. Not only was Riley Finnegan insanely gorgeous and smart, but she was probably also the most confident, self-assured fourteen-year-old girl on the East Coast. No wonder why Riley wasn't jealous that Matt was hanging out with Nola. She didn't seem to have an insecure bone in her body. Come to think of it, if Nola had the looks and personality of Riley Finnegan, she wouldn't feel insecure, either.

"So what do you have to eat around here?" Matt

asked, snapping Nola out of her trance. "Arugula? Kale? I'm famished."

Nola blinked a few times and steadied herself. "Um, well, I, uh . . . usually make some Chex Party Mix," she stammered.

"*Viva la* Chex Party Mix!" Matt cheered, tossing his phone onto her bed. "Let's hit the kitchen."

"You go ahead, I'll be right down," Nola said.

"Okay, but hurry up. I don't want Ian taking me into the interrogation room so he can practice more of his bad-cop routine," he said, smirking.

As soon as Matt left, Nola tried to quell an ominous feeling that was bubbling up inside her. She kept eyeing Matt's phone as if it were a bomb that she had to disarm or else everyone in Poughkeepsie would die. No matter how much she willed herself to ignore this feeling, she couldn't.

Nola quickly grabbed Matt's phone and went into his sent text messages folder. She scrolled down to the most recent one and opened it up. Nola dropped the phone back onto her comforter and recoiled from it as if it were radioactive. But no matter how far she retreated, Nola wouldn't be able to erase these two words from her mind.

LUV YA

She raced to her bathroom and washed her hands vigorously, hoping that scrubbing them like a surgeon would somehow change what had just happened. As she lathered up, Nola's thoughts went directly to the slide show on Riley's profile, which she'd only seen about nine seconds of. There were two pictures of Matt and Riley at Rooney Fest and in one of them, Matt was kissing Riley on the side of her face, right above her ear. Riley appeared to be in the middle of a laugh, her mouth open and her eyes squinting.

When Nola turned off the faucet and dried her hands, she realized that a week from now, Riley would be in Poughkeepsie, glued to the side of her temporary best friend/*only* guy on her crush list. A knot formed in the pit of her stomach.

Nola wasn't one to ignore her gut feelings, but she tried to as she bounded down the stairs. She just didn't want to believe that she and Matt would be all downhill from here.

# Chapter 13

On the way home from bowling last night, Dane had told Marnie that their Friday double date with Lizette and Sawyer was going to take place at Tucker McFadden's "Aloha, Poughkeepsie!" luau. Marnie hadn't been able to contain her glee. It was undoubtedly the most exclusive party of the season and attending it with her fellow Majors would definitely put Marnie at the center of the best gossip in school. Not only that, but it would definitely help get her back on track after that weird freakout at the bowling alley. Earlier today Marnie had written a top ten list of reasons to forget about Nola and move on. This ranked at number one: *Because your fate as a Major depends on it.*

Now that Marnie was strolling toward Tucker's gigantic Tudor-style home on a quiet cul-de-sac, her anti-Nola list was far from her mind. In fact, Marnie was so giddy about where she was and how she looked that she almost squealed. Marnie was wearing an aqua-colored Joie cropped cardigan over a white lacy tank, with a Diesel gray corduroy micro-mini and a pair of bronze round-toed flats from Bandolino. She felt ultra-confident in this outfit because it had been handpicked by the ultimate fashion icon, Lizette Levin.

After school today, Lizette and Marnie had raided Erin's room and nabbed the best stuff they could find. In fact, they'd had such a great time tearing her sister's closet apart in a Go Girl Energy Drink fueled frenzy that Marnie hadn't bothered asking Lizette why she skipped the student council meeting yesterday afternoon. Lizette hadn't seemed upset or anything, so did it even matter?

"You could wait up for us, you know!" a boy's voice shouted from a few feet behind.

Marnie turned around and watched Dane as he took long strides up the driveway, while behind him Lizette and Sawyer kept a snail's pace. Marnie smiled as Dane jogged up to her. He looked so incredible tonight. A pair of faded Hudson jeans hugged his frame in a way his khakis never could. He pushed up the sleeves of his black half-zip sweater and then glanced at his silver Fossil watch.

"What's the rush?" Dane asked when he finally caught up to Marnie.

"Sorry, I guess I'm just excited." Marnie took both of Dane's hands in hers and grinned.

He pulled her in a little closer. "Excited about what?" he asked softly.

"Being here with you and Lizette," Marnie said, trying to quell her enthusiasm so that she didn't seem childish.

"Don't forget Sawyer," Dane added as he kissed her on the cheek.

*Oh, yeah. Sawyer.*

When Lizette mentioned this "let's hang out with our boys" idea, Marnie had been a little worried that it would be weird seeing her friend all cozy with the guy she'd been infatuated with since middle school. But as Sawyer and Lizette approached with their arms around each other's waists, Marnie realized just how perfect they looked together.

Sawyer was rocking his traditional skater threads — baggy cargo pants that hung super-low, a long-sleeve T-shirt with a flame design running up from the hem, and gray canvas sneakers. His straight dark hair was thick with pomade and sticking up in several directions. Tonight, Lizette was his mirror image, decked out in plaid board shorts with a vintage 70s halter top and Michael Kors sandals that laced up to her knees. Her locks were wavy and a tad frizzy, as if she'd just come from the beach.

But what really caught Marnie's attention was how both of them had this "I'm so freaking *smexy*" swagger. Even if Marnie *wanted* to be with Sawyer (which she didn't, of course), she'd have to learn how to walk with that swagger, too.

"How disappointing," Lizette said as she took in the sight of Tucker's luxurious crib. "I thought there'd be at least a four-car garage."

Marnie rolled her eyes and giggled. Only Lizette would be blasé about the awesomeness of the McFadden residence.

Sawyer let go of Lizette's waist and jammed his hand in his left pocket. He pulled out a pack of cigarettes, inspected the contents, and then hid them away again. "Well, Zee, I'm sure a dip in the Jacuzzi will more than make up for it."

"I brought my bikini." Lizette happily tapped her light brown whip-stitched Chloe shoulder satchel, but frowned when she met Marnie's gaze. "You didn't bring yours, did you?"

"Sorry, I'm much too pale to be flaunting my flesh in front of half the school," Marnie said.

"What a shame," Dane said impishly.

Lizette bounded up to the door and rang the bell. "There better be plenty to drink."

Marnie eyes grew wide. *Drink? As in* drink-drink? Sure, Marnie had heard rumors about Lizette's European partying, but that was before Marnie had gotten to know her. Lizette had never mentioned *anything* about an interest in drinking to Marnie before.

"Of course, there will be," Dane said nonchalantly. "This is Tucker we're talking about. He always throws ragers."

*Wait, now Dane is all about drinking?*

Gossip about Dane's dual bad-boy identity had circulated around school, too, but Marnie just thought he was the type of guy that liked being popular, so he'd go to parties with the sole purpose of charming everyone, not getting wasted. What if she'd been mistaken?

The door flew open and there stood the richest and greasiest seventeen-year-old boy in all of Dutchess County, dressed in a red Hawaiian shirt, wearing a pair of Oakley sunglasses, and holding a bunch of colorful leis in his hand.

"Aloha, friends," Tucker said, his round cheeks rosy. "Welcome to paradise."

*Good lord.*

Dane walked in first and shook Tucker's hand. "Thanks for having us over, bro."

"*Daaaaayyyyyyyyne,* my right-hand man," Tucker gurgled as he placed a yellow lei over Dane's head. "The party is just gettin' started, dawg. As usual, you can raid the libations."

*Right-hand man? As usual?*

This evening was getting more and more interesting by the second.

Marnie tried to follow Dane into the foyer and avoid getting breathed on by Tucker, but the host of the party wouldn't let her slip by. "And who do have we here?" he asked, blocking her passage.

"Marnie Fitzpatrick," she replied.

"I know we just met," Tucker said through a giddy chuckle. "But I have to *lei* you."

"Wow, that was . . . clever," Marnie said as Tucker slipped a red lei around her neck.

Thankfully, Dane didn't waste any time taking Marnie by the hand and leading her down the marble-floored hallway while Lizette and Sawyer engaged in more witty banter with Tucker. Marnie glanced around at all the high-profile upperclassmen who were crowding the house. A week ago, she would have felt so psyched to be in their presence, hoping to get noticed. But now people were nodding in Marnie's direction, acknowledging her as one of their own and as if she'd always belonged.

*This is freaking incredible!*

Dane stopped once he reached the center of the elegant living room, where most of the bodies were mingling around sleek modern style furniture. Tucker had his iPod hooked up to the stereo system and a Kanye West song was filtering through the air. Marnie kept looking around for Lizette and Sawyer, but she didn't see them.

"Pretty great, isn't it?" Dane said, rubbing the base of her back softly.

Marnie nodded. "Yeah, Tucker's house is amazing. I've never seen a stone fireplace that gigantic before."

"Wanna drink?"

Marnie wasn't about to feel pressured into drinking — even if it was Dane — so she took a deep breath and said, "Actually, could you get me a Diet Coke?"

"You bet. Diet Coke and what?" Dane asked as he checked out the crowd.

Okay, now Marnie was feeling a little pressure. If Lizette were here, she'd know exactly how to finesse this situation and not look like a freshman reject. But since her friend was MIA — *again* — Marnie would have to brave this awkward moment herself. "Diet Coke and some . . . ice?"

Dane laughed and kissed her earlobe. "I meant, what else do you want mixed in, silly."

*Duh, I* know!

Marnie bit her lip in a small attempt to stall. If she just played along with Dane and held on to the cup all night, maybe he wouldn't even notice that she wasn't drinking? That way, Marnie could appear to be . . . whatever it was Dane wanted her be, and no one would be the wiser. "Rum would be good," Marnie blurted out.

Dane tapped her on the tip of her nose with his finger. "Coming right up."

When he wove his way through the crowd, Marnie mentally patted herself on the back.

*I am* such *a genius!*

Then she felt a quick hip-check.

It was purple-lei Lizette, already holding a blue plastic cup, and green-lei Sawyer, hands in his pockets.

"Omigod, Marnie, you should see the Jacuzzi," Lizette said, clearly impressed. "It practically takes up the whole deck."

And Marnie was supposed to care because . . . ?

"Where'd Dane go?" Sawyer asked, leaning back on his heels and peering out into the mob.

"Oh, he went to get me a drink," Marnie replied.

Lizette took a long sip out of her cup and then held it out to Marnie. "Here, have some of mine."

Marnie bit her lip again. At the moment, she didn't have a genius plan that would help her pull one over on Lizette. There was only way to deal, and that was to lie.

"You know what? I think I'm coming down with something." Marnie faked a few coughs for emphasis. "I'd hate to give you my germs."

Lizette raised her eyebrows, as if she knew exactly what Marnie was up to. But instead of letting it slide or telling Marnie not to worry, Lizette rolled her eyes and heaved an exasperated sigh. She turned to Sawyer, held out her cup, and said, "Hey, can you hold on to this for me while I go change into my swimsuit?"

Sawyer said nothing, but took the cup anyway.

And then for the second time in two days, Lizette bailed on Marnie, just when she needed her. However, at least in this situation, she had the courtesy to snub Marnie to her face.

Speaking of faces, Marnie's was turning as red as the lei around her neck. She shifted her position a bit so that she was standing beside Sawyer. This way, he wouldn't be able to see the shame in her eyes.

They stood there silent for a minute, gazing at their fellow classmates as if they were people-watching at a sidewalk café.

"You know what this reminds me of?" Sawyer said out of the blue.

Marnie stood on her tiptoes as she scanned the room for Dane. "No. What?"

Sawyer sniffed the contents of Lizette's cup and then smirked. "Brian Bennington's fourth-grade birthday party."

Marnie's eyes lit up with recognition. She'd been at that party! It was years ago, but she remembered it vividly because it was held at Chuck E. Cheese. Marnie had stalked Sawyer from PacMan to Street Fighter, but she had no idea he knew she was there.

"Remember when Brian's mom yelled at you for beaning him with one of those plastic balls in the pit?" Marnie asked, giggling.

Sawyer spun around so fast that he startled Marnie. "Hold on. That was payback."

Marnie shook her head a bit when she noticed she was staring into Sawyer's almost-black almond-shaped eyes. "And what did Brian do to warrant such vengeance?"

"He pantsed me in gym class," Sawyer said, as if he was recalling it fondly. "But in all fairness, that was just retaliation for when I emptied out his Johnson's Baby Shampoo bottle and refilled it with honey."

Marnie nearly doubled over in laughter. "So *that's* why Brian came to school with a shaved head."

Sawyer ran a hand through his hair. "Yeah, but for some reason, he went around telling everyone he had lice, which wasn't much better than the truth."

"He was ostracized for days. Didn't he have to eat lunch with —"

"Lou the Janitor?" Sawyer finished Marnie's thought. "Afraid so. But they're still very close. Isn't that nice?"

Marnie couldn't stop smiling. She had been so afraid to talk with Sawyer for the longest time, but it was all for nothing. He was incredibly easygoing and funny and sweet.

And getting cuter by the second.

"So are you going to join Lizette in the Jacuzzi?" she asked. Marnie bowed her head. Had that sounded as dirty as she thought it did?

"Nah, I'm cool like you, Marnie. Keeping the flesh under wraps."

Sawyer had just traveled from cute to head of the hotness committee at the speed of light.

Marnie felt a tap on her shoulder.

"They just had regular Coke." Dane was standing next to her, holding two cups in his hands and grinning.

"That's fine." Marnie took her cup and smiled back graciously.

Sawyer set Lizette's drink on an end table and looked at his watch. "Guess I should go check on Zee."

Marnie could have sworn she felt a pang of disappointment just then. "I'd watch out for Brian Bennington if I were you."

Sawyer covered his mouth when he laughed, which Marnie thought was adorable. "Feel better," he said before drifting off into the throngs of people pressed together all around them.

Dane handed his cup to Marnie and looked at her with concern. "Are you okay?"

Marnie had no idea how to answer that question, especially when Dane brought her in for a hug and she watched Sawyer walk away over his shoulder.

**nolaj1994:** *hey there*
**mheatherly:** *hi! whazzup, miss james?*
**nolaj1994:** *nothing, just wanted to say thx again for coming over last nite*
**mheatherly:** *no thx necessary. we're BFF remember?*
**nolaj1994:** *i remember* ☺
**mheatherly:** *anyway, i had a great time*
**nolaj1994:** *u did?*
**mheatherly:** *of course. the best part was when Ian ambushed us under the "do u want some cookies & milk?" guise*
**nolaj1994:** *ugh, i know. he has issues*
**mheatherly:** *so what r u up to today? making cool jewelry?*
**nolaj1994:** *i think i'm going 2 lay off the jewelry making 4 a while*
**mheatherly:** *oh, no, u don't*
**nolaj1994:** *what?*
**mheatherly:** *u can't let a bad experience affect something u luv 2 do*
**nolaj1994:** *i know, but i just don't feel up 2 it*
**mheatherly:** *maybe u just need some inspiration*
**mheatherly:** *whenever i get stuck on a song or can't figure out a chord progression i try 2 do something that will open up the channels of creativity*

**nolaj1994:** *how do u do that?*

**mheatherly:** *that, my friend, is what i intend 2 show u*

**nolaj1994:** *it doesn't involve anything . . . sketchy, does it?*

**mheatherly:** *again with the "sketchy" remark. r u trying to tell me something?*

**nolaj1994:** *no, of course not*

**mheatherly:** *ok, so u'll meet up with me then?*

**nolaj1994:** *sure. where/when?*

**mheatherly:** *i'll text u in a bit. just have to figure out the logistics*

**nolaj1994:** *ok, ttyl*

**mheatherly:** *yep, bye!*

# Chapter 14

If Nola had known that Matt's method of finding his inspiration involved taking the city bus to an area of Poughkeepsie that could be best described as the "tenement district," she probably would have stayed home and watched the Cartoon Network all day long. But alas, she had been swept up in the idea of going someplace — *any* place — with Matt, and judging by her ghetto-fied surroundings, it might have been the last poor decision Nola would ever get to make.

As she and Matt ambled down a street with several boarded-up stores and graffiti-covered apartment buildings, Nola's eyes darted around, looking out for suspicious individuals carrying lead pipes or switchblades or other concealable weapons that they could use to maim and/or kill them.

"So this is probably your definition of sketchy, huh?" Matt was obviously aware of how uncomfortable Nola was in this dodgy neighborhood.

Actually, Nola was so concerned about their safety that she had spent virtually no time thinking about how cute Matt looked in his dingy Army jacket and his worn-in black jeans with a gaping hole in the knee.

"Shhh . . . they can hear you," Nola whispered as

she buttoned up her heavy gray wool cardigan. The late September wind was giving way to chillier temperatures. She'd have to fish out her fall jacket *if* she got home in one piece.

Matt shot Nola a peculiar look. "Um, who are *they*?"

"I don't know exactly," Nola replied cagily.

"Right," he said. "Well, try not to let on that you're crazy when we get there, okay?"

"Where is *there* anyway?" Nola's heart began to work overtime when she considered the worst possible theory — Matt's inspiration was due to some underground street drug, and they were going to meet his supplier in a tawdry back-alley crack house. It would explain the suspension from Arlington that Marnie had warned her about, wouldn't it? And why his mother seemed to be out of the picture, too.

*God, Nol. You've been watching way too much* Veronica Mars.

Matt made a sharp right-hand turn down a narrow alley, and Nola almost swallowed her wintergreen-flavored gum. Matt walked over to the side door of a brick building and knocked. "*Here* is there," he said to Nola with a wink.

*Please don't be a drug dealer, please don't be a drug dealer,* Nola chanted in her head.

When the door opened, a man the size of a tank

with a bushy mustache and an elaborate tattoo of a saint on his upper arm appeared before them.

*Oh, crap.*

*"¿Como estás, Chico?"* Matt raised his hand in the air as if he was waiting for a high-five.

*"Muy bien,"* Chico said through a big, warm laugh. He gripped Matt's hand and pulled him in for a chest bump. *"¿Qué pasa?"*

Matt glanced over at Nola and smiled. "Just wanted to show this young lady around. That okay?"

*"Por supuesto."* Chico grinned and held the door wide open for them.

"You rule, Chico." Matt waved at Nola. "Come on."

Nola looked at him apprehensively. "You know, it's getting kind of late," she said, hoping that if she stalled enough she could figure out if Chico had been on last week's episode of *America's Most Wanted*.

"Nola, it's four o'clock. The early-bird specials at Palace Diner aren't even being served yet," Matt joked.

Nola pulled her sleeves up to make sure her itchy skin was the result of wearing just a T-shirt underneath her wool sweater. No such luck. Red blotches were forming in the creases of her elbows. Any minute now she'd be covered in hives and totally humiliated.

But before she could contemplate an escape route, Matt took Nola's hand in his and held it tightly. Then his other hand touched her chin, and he guided her face upward so she could look directly into his gorgeous, soulful hazel eyes. Nola had never wanted to freeze-frame a moment more than this one.

When Matt simply said, "Don't worry," Nola instantly felt at ease. She had no idea what kind of powers Matt was using on her, and right now she didn't really care.

Without letting go of her hand, Matt wove his way down a steep staircase. With each step, Nola heard the sound of music echoing louder and louder. As soon as they got to the bottom, Matt pushed through a swinging door and suddenly, Nola was standing in front of a live mariachi band being led by a boy who didn't seem much older than she was. And in the back, strumming a guitar, was a tall, lanky man who bore a striking resemblance to her understudy best friend, Matt Heatherly.

"That's my dad!" Matt shouted over the music, pointing to the man in question.

"I know!"

Nola couldn't believe it. Matt brought her all the way to wherever the hell they were, so she could meet his *father*? Wasn't that a *ginormous* flashing neon sign indicating that he *liked* her liked her? Why else would he do such a thing?

"When I want to get inspired, this is what I do. I listen to my dad play." Matt was so proud that his face was shining. "Aren't they freaking incredible?"

Nola had to admit, the band was great. Her feet were tapping along in time with their infectious Latin music like they did when she'd listen to Los Lonely Boys.

"Juan is a whiz kid," Matt screamed into Nola's ear. "He's the only one from his family who managed to flee from Cuba. My dad took Juan on as his student last year, and he mastered the vihuela in a few months because he practiced for five hours every single day. Now tell me *that* doesn't inspire you."

Nola stared at Juan as he effortlessly strummed his high-pitched twelve-string guitar. She could see by the intense look on his face that he was passionate about his craft, and that he didn't take his musical gift for granted. She recognized this look because she'd seen it on Matt's face before, when she watched that video of him performing at Rooney Fest. She also recognized this look because she'd seen it on her own face, too, when she caught a glimpse of herself in a hazy reflection off the living-room window while beading Marnie's bracelet. She hadn't known what that expression meant back then, but she did now, because of Matt.

Instinctively, Nola reached out and took Matt's hand. He turned his head and gave her one of his heart-stopping smiles. She would have said something then, if she hadn't gotten choked up by the wave of strong feelings that had just swelled inside of her. Lucky for Nola, Matt knew what was on the tip of her tongue.

"You're welcome," he said as the music played on.

Two hours and three amazing sets later, Matt and Nola sat dumbstruck at Stewart's Ice Cream Shoppe, staring at the mother of all banana splits that just been put before them. The sundae was so gigantic that the wait-ress had to carry it over to their table with two hands. Nola licked her lips in anticipation — she hadn't eaten all day, and digging into this plate of vanilla-chocolate-strawberry splendor would be the cherry on top of her inspiring afternoon. She couldn't wait to get home and start working on her next creation.

Matt grabbed his spoon and carved out a large chunk of banana from the bottom of the sundae. "If your mom saw you ingesting this right now, what would she do?"

"I'm not sure." Nola savored the creamy flavor of whipped topping before going for a spoonful of choco-late ice cream. "But whatever punishment I got would be well worth it."

"Punished for eating ice cream," Matt said, shaking his head. "It's a cruel world, Nol."

Nola smiled as she took another bite of the sundae. When Matt suggested they stop somewhere for a "nosh," this was the only place she could think of. But as they rode the bus into town, Nola had had second thoughts. Stewart's was her and Marnie's favorite hangout spot, where they'd spent hours talking and nibbling on waffle cones. She thought it might feel weird being there with Matt. But on the contrary, Nola was so comfortable with him by her side, she was able to put any memories of Marnie out of her mind.

That is, until Matt brought up the girl.

"So, we're past the three-day warranty," Matt said as he wiped some caramel syrup off his chin with a napkin. "Are you going to keep me around as your Marnie substitute, or are you going to cut your losses and run?"

Nola sighed. After Matt had taken her to see his father perform today, she'd hoped that he wasn't being nice to her out of obligation. In fact, she'd hoped that their day together meant something much more to him. However, now that Matt mentioned their little "arrangement," Nola was worried that she'd misread his actions and intentions.

"I haven't decided yet," she mumbled as she plunged

her spoon into the untouched scoop of strawberry ice cream.

"Maybe we haven't put my best-friend skills to the ultimate test," Matt said.

Nola furrowed her brow. *What is he getting at?*

Matt could see that she was bewildered. "Allow me to explain."

"Please do."

"The way I see it, I have excelled in two out of three critical categories. One, the Friday night non-sleepover. Two, the unexpected field trip to the ne'er-do-well section of Poughkeepsie, where music mix the bourgeoisie and the rebel."

Nola almost spit out her rainbow-colored sprinkles. "Did you just quote *Madonna*?"

"What? I own *one* Madge album." He grinned. "Are you going to call the heterosexual male police on me?"

As soon as he said that, Nola wanted to lean across the table and kiss his cool, sweet lips. "And the third category is . . . ?"

"Can you keep a secret?"

"Sure. What?" Nola replied.

Matt chuckled and skimmed his spoon along the edge of the plate in search of stray peanuts. "No, I mean that's the third category. We haven't told each other a secret yet."

All of a sudden, Nola felt as though her chest was being constricted by a Victorian-age corset.

"Okay, your face is turning blue. Either your airway is blocked or you don't trust me. Which is it? Because I need to warm up before I perform the Heimlich." Matt stretched his arms in front of him and wiggled his fingers.

Nola crumpled up her napkin and tossed it at him. "What kind of secret do you want me to tell you?"

Matt ran his hand through his shaggy hair, a move that made Nola feel as wobbly as the uneven leg on their table. "How am I supposed to know? I'm not a chick."

"Whatever, Material Girl," Nola giggled.

Matt's eyes grew wide as he laughed at her sarcastic remark. "All right, Miss James, why don't you tell me who your *secret* crush is?"

Nola didn't need a mirror to know that her face had gone from blue to stark white. She opened her mouth to say something, but all that came out was a noise that sounded like a cross between a cough and a whistle.

"Come on, I'm your understudy best friend. I won't tell a soul," Matt nudged her.

*Oh, my god, I'm going to actually* die *of embarrassment.*

Nola scrambled for words. "Um . . . you wouldn't know the guy. He lives in . . . Iraq."

*What the hell? Why did I say* Iraq?!

Matt sat back in his chair and examined Nola scrupulously. "Is he a soldier or an insurgent?"

Nola wanted to laugh, but she was too busy trying to dig herself out of the king-size hole she was in. "He's . . . an exchange student."

"Okay, let's try this again," he said. "Same idea. Different topic. Have you ever done anything . . . *illegal?*"

Nola was finally able to exhale. At least they were on to another subject that didn't involve her professing her secret love for Matt. She was almost overjoyed to answer this question.

"Last year, I got caught shoplifting thongs from Victoria's Secret at the Galleria," she spat out.

Matt laughed so hard that he practically fell out of his chair. "I pegged you as a high-rise brief type of girl."

*What was* that *supposed to mean?*

"My underwear is not up for discussion," she snapped.

"Nola, I believe the crush-on-an-exchange-student-in-Iraq story more than I believe this one."

"It's true!" she said adamantly.

Matt stared her down so hard that Nola knew she had to recant part of the story.

"Okay, I *personally* didn't steal from Victoria's Secret," Nola admitted. "Marnie did. But I was there when it happened!"

"So you were an *accessory* to thong stealing?" Matt asked skeptically.

"Not exactly," she said.

"Not *exactly*," Matt repeated.

Nola knew she was going to regret this, but she had no other choice. "I'm the reason she got caught."

Matt's mouth fell open.

Her heart started racing so fast her brain couldn't keep up with it. "Marnie was so upset about her parents separating and money was already tight and I went to take her shopping to cheer her up but all it did was make her sadder and then I saw her grab some thongs and put them in her purse and when we headed toward the door an employee stopped us and before she could say anything I . . . I . . ."

"You what?"

"I started . . . crying," she said flatly.

Matt put his hand to his forehead. "Oh, no."

"You can't tell *anyone*," Nola said, her voice shaking with fear. "The only person who knows about the Thong Thief incident is Marnie's mom. She had to come pick us up from mall security."

"Relax, Nola. I promise to take Marnie's thong story to the grave," Matt said, crossing his heart.

Nola moved the banana split to the side and put her head down on the table. "Thank you," she muttered.

"You'll feel better once I tell you a secret," she heard him say as he patted her on the head. "Ask me anything."

*This is my chance to find out if he was suspended, or whether his mother moved out of the house.*

Nola lifted her head up a bit and saw Matt smiling at her. His eyes were twinkling like usual, but there was something else she hadn't noticed before. Nola could see how much trust he had in her, and for some reason, the only way she felt good about uncovering Matt's secrets was if he volunteered that information simply because he wanted to confide in her, not because he wanted to pass some silly best-friend test.

"So, do you think your dad liked me?"

"Actually, Nola," Matt said, smirking, "I think he loved you."

The discrepancy between the size of the smile on Nola's face and the size of the smile in Nola's heart could not be measured by modern scientific methods. Nola was about to look down before her grin betrayed her, but the sight of two blonde girls standing outside the window caught her by surprise. One of them was wearing a vintage denim jacket, the other had on a bright red poncho, and both of them were beleaguered with shopping bags.

As much as she wanted to hide, Nola couldn't stop

staring at Marnie and Lizette, or wondering what they were laughing so hard about. When Marnie turned around and spotted her sitting there with Matt, the first thing Nola noticed was the stern expression on Marnie's face. She stood there, gawking at Nola in pure contempt, for what seemed like hours. Finally, Marnie tugged on Lizette's hand and gestured in Nola's direction. Lizette squinted for a second, then her eyes bulged when she met Nola's gaze.

When they hurried off together down the street and out of sight, Nola shoved another spoonful of banana split into her mouth. But it didn't taste good anymore.

# Chapter 15

This Weekend's Highlights (and Unfortunately, Lowlights)

HIGHLIGHT: Slow-dancing with Dane to Natasha Bedingfield in the center of Tucker's living room. Everyone clapped when the song was over and we kissed. Talk about a romantic spectacle! Boo-freaking-yah!

LOWLIGHT: Watching Sawyer put Dane and Zee in a cab because they were too tipsy to walk home. Thankfully, when Mom picked me up, she was so thrilled that I was even at Tucker's mansion party that she didn't ask a lot of annoying questions (which is a highlight within a lowlight).

HIGHLIGHT: Saturday's shopping spree with Zee. We hit the Galleria so hard, the place might never recover!

LOWLIGHT: The shopping spree was Zee's mea culpa for having too many mystery drinks and ignoring me all night after telling me that my eye makeup was sort of cheap-looking. (Ouch.)

ULTRA-LOWLIGHT: Seeing Nola at Stewart's. As if facing (a.k.a. avoiding) her in English class Monday through Friday isn't enough cruelty!

Early on Sunday afternoon, Marnie was standing near the counter at East Garden Chinese Restaurant, waiting for the takeout order she and her mom had placed by phone an hour ago. It was a gorgeous late September day — sixty-eight degrees, no clouds, light breeze — so she offered to stroll the eleven blocks and pick up their shrimp lo mein and sesame chicken herself. But even though the bright sun had put her in a good mood, Marnie was growing more and more impatient as other people traipsed in and received their orders while she lurked off to the side, wondering if someone actually had gone to China to cook her lunch.

"Troy! Garlic beef and broccoli!" a small Asian man called out as he wiped his hands on his stained apron.

A round-faced boy wearing a Vassar sweatshirt grabbed a large paper bag and bolted out the door.

*What the hell? I've been here* way *longer than him!*

Marnie sighed when she realized that staring at the tall Asian man working the wok wasn't going to make her order appear any sooner. However, distracting herself with her cell phone seemed like a better way to kill time. Marnie flipped open her phone and scrolled through the pictures she took at Tucker's luau. She giggled at the one of her and Dane sticking their tongues out at each other, as well as a photo of a bikini-clad Lizette wading in the Jacuzzi and vamping at the camera with Hannah Dobson and Skylar Brooks — two beautiful juniors who ruled the upper echelon of Poughkeepsie Central and looked as though they belonged on *Laguna Beach*.

But when Marnie looked closer at the Jacuzzi jpeg, Marnie noticed that Sawyer Lee was captured in the background. Actually, it was just one of his arms — he must have been sauntering off somewhere while Lizette laughed it up with her new party pals. Still, the sight of Sawyer's toned bicep made Marnie's heart throb. She took her pinky finger and ran it down Sawyer's forearm, pausing for a second when she heard her name called out.

*Finally!*

Marnie shut her cell phone and glanced up, expecting to see the short Asian guy holding a paper bag. And there was an Asian guy standing before her, just not the one behind the counter.

"I hope you ordered the moo shu chicken," Sawyer said as he held his skateboard underneath the arm that Marnie had just been ogling in the photo. He looked as though he'd just competed in the Gravity Games — his cheeks were flushed and his olive-colored skin was glistening a bit. Saywer's long brown shorts were hanging off his hips and when he yanked them up, Marnie saw that he was wearing fingerless gloves and had painted his nails black.

In all the years that Marnie had gawked at him from afar, Sawyer had never, *ever* looked hotter.

Marnie put her phone back into the red hobo bag that she'd picked up at Urban Behavior yesterday and reminded herself that standing in front of her was not just Sawyer Lee, but her friend's lovah-man. That's right — *lovah-man.*

"Nope, I ordered the sesame chicken," she said plainly.

Sawyer wiped his forehead with the back of his hand while Marnie fought hard not to gasp. "Too bad. You're missing out on their best dish."

"Oh, well. I'll just have to wait until next time." She tugged at the bottom of her green Heritage T-shirt from Abercrombie so that it fit more snugly around her chest.

*Ugh, stop doing that!*

Sawyer pointed to the table in the corner. "Not necessarily. You can have some of mine."

Marnie's heart did a back handspring. The former number-one stud on her crush list was asking her to hang out with him!

"Come on, there's no way I'm going to finish all that," he said, nodding in the direction of his huge meal.

Marnie grinned. "I suppose taking a few bites wouldn't ruin my appetite."

They walked over to the table and sat down. Sawyer

kept his skateboard on his lap while he opened up containers of food and handed Marnie some plastic utensils. Marnie dug right into the moo shu chicken and smiled the moment she tasted it.

"Pretty good, huh?" Sawyer asked while drizzling duck sauce over his egg roll.

Marnie went for second helpings. "Wow, I might have to change my order. If it ever shows up, that is."

"Wait, who answered the phone when you called to place the order?"

Marnie peered at Sawyer curiously. "I have no clue."

Sawyer took a sip of his soda. "Did the guy say 'East Garden, how may I help you?' or 'Hello, Chinese restaurant?'"

"'Hello, Chinese restaurant,' I think," Marnie said.

"Aha," Sawyer said knowingly. "You better double-check that they got your order."

"Why?"

"Because you spoke with Cheng, not Chen," Sawyer explained. "Cheng is quite forgetful whereas Chen remembers everything."

Marnie grinned again as she tore a piece off a moo shu pancake. "And you know this how?"

"Didn't you hear, Marnie? All of us Poughkeepsie Asians are related." Sawyer winked.

Marnie kicked him under the table. "Shut up."

Sawyer chuckled. "Seriously, I've been burned by Cheng enough times to know to follow up on him."

"So you're a regular here?" Marnie stared into Sawyer's dark eyes while chanting "Zee" and "Dane" in her head.

"Yeah, I am. In fact, when I haven't come by or placed an order for delivery in a while, Chen will call my cell phone to see if I'm still alive," Sawyer said, smiling.

"That's sweet." Marnie thought of the message Dane had left her on Saturday morning — *Sorry for not walking you home, cutie. I just got a little carried away last night. Talk soon!* Marnie had returned his call, but he never picked up, and she hadn't heard from him today, either. Marnie considered calling Dane again to make sure he was alive, but that would mean bailing on Sawyer and she didn't want to do that just yet.

"Know what else is sweet?" Sawyer said with a mouthful of white rice.

"What?"

"Moldy bread."

*Maybe leaving now isn't such a bad idea.*

"Moldy bread?" Marnie repeated. She set her fork down and leaned back in her chair, preparing for a quick getaway.

Sawyer covered his mouth as he laughed. "Don't look at me. It was *your* science project."

Marnie glared at Sawyer teasingly. "So *you're* the one who stole my fourth-grade bacteria experiment! I always wondered who snatched it right before the fair."

"I'm really sorry," Sawyer said. "But Brian Bennington triple-dog-dared me. I couldn't back down."

"Well, I got an F, Sawyer. I hope you can live with that on your conscience," Marnie said, flicking some cabbage at him with her fork.

"I don't know. Can you live with sending me to the doctor with botulism?" Sawyer replied with a smirk.

Marnie crossed her arms in front of her chest. "You can't get botulism from eating moldy bread."

"And you know this how?"

"Because it was *my science project,* dweeb!"

Sawyer was laughing so hard now that he could barely breathe.

"Marnie! Shrimp lo mein and sesame chicken!" Chen (or Cheng) shouted.

Marnie pushed herself away from the table and marched over to the counter to pick up her bag of food. Even though Sawyer had pulled a mean stunt years ago, Marnie couldn't muster up a shred of anger. In fact, she was practically aglow with happiness. Sawyer Lee had remembered her moldy bread all this time, and here Marnie had thought she was completely invisible to him.

But now, there wasn't much she could do about it.

When Marnie got her change back from the cashier, she turned around and saw Sawyer standing so close to her that if she reached out, she could touch him.

"Would it make you feel any better if I gave you my lucky numbers?" Sawyer handed her the small strip of paper that was in his fortune cookie and scratched the back of his neck as he waited for Marnie to respond.

"Maybe," Marnie said, clutching the paper tightly in her hand.

*Easy, girl. Dane is your amazing kinda, sorta boyfriend, and Sawyer is Zee's, which means COMPLETELY OFF-LIMITS!*

"Just don't tell Zee if you win the lotto with those," Sawyer added.

"I won't," Marnie replied as she shoved the paper into her pocket. "I better take off before the food gets cold."

"Right," he said, stepping out of her way. "It was nice talking with you, Marnie. You're pretty cool."

The second she got home, Marnie handed the bag from East Garden to her mom and ran up to her room. She pulled the paper out of her pocket, scanned the lucky numbers, and then flipped it over to read Sawyer's fortune.

*Resist any further temptation.*

Sunday, September 23, 3:17 P.M.

**You are invited to a conference.**
**queenzee signed on**
**2kool4skool signed on**
**grierrox signed on**
**marniebird signed on**
**grierrox:** *I luv conferences!!!*
**marniebird:** *so do i! how r u guys?*
**queenzee:** *good. we're @ brynne's, testing her dad's latest shipment of laptops. u should see the all the smoking threads she got in nyc!*
**marniebird:** *nyc? when did you go there?*
**2kool4skool:** *monday afternoon, my mom took me, zee, and grier to this killer sample sale at her friend's boutique in the east village*
**marniebird:** *oh*
**grierrox:** *u had that student council thing, m. that sux*
**marniebird:** *that's ok, zee and i went shopping yesterday*
**queenzee:** *yeah, but we didn't find anything as nice as brynne's booty*
**marniebird:** *brynne's what?*
**2kool4skool:** *booty = treasure. *sigh* how can u not know that, miss i'm running for class treasurer?*
**grierrox:** *LOL, i thought zee was talking about brynne's badunkadunk!*

**marniebird:** *me 2*

**queenzee:** *do anything fun today, marn?*

**marniebird:** *no*

**2kool4skool:** *that's not surprising*

**grierrox:** *u should b here with us!*

**marniebird:** *actually, i'm just mellowing out from Tucker's party*

**2kool4skool:** *um, why? zee said it sucked*

**marniebird:** *really? i thought u had a good time, zee*

**queenzee:** *it was ok*

**marniebird:** *well i had a blast, it was so great of dane to get us in!*

**queenzee:** *i guess*

**2kool4skool:** *i heard dane got plastered and was hitting on every girl at the party*

**marniebird:** *that is so false. he was with me all night*

**grierrox:** *well, i want to hear more about sawyer*

**marniebird:** *what about him?*

**queenzee:** *oh, i was just telling the girls about our naughty makeout session in the master bedroom* ☺

**marniebird:** *eek! this is the first i'm hearing of it!*

**queenzee:** *sorry, it just slipped my mind*

**2kool4skool:** *how can u forget something like rolling around on a bed with sawyer lee?*

**queenzee:** *i know! impossible*

**grierrox:** *oh, no! we're missing beauty and the geek!*

**2kool4skool:** *ugh, my Tivo is still busted. we should go*
**queenzee:** *ttyl, marn*
**grierrox:** *bye! xo*
**marniebird:** *c ya!*

**2kool4skool signed off**
**grierrox signed off**

**queenzee:** *oh, 1 more thing*
**marniebird:** *yeah?*
**queenzee:** *could u ask dane if he found my earring? it might have come off in the cab*
**marniebird:** *sure*
**queenzee:** *thx, they're my favs!*
**marniebird:** *hope he has it then*
**queenzee:** *l8ter*
**marniebird:** *l8ter*

# Chapter 16

As Nola sat in Mr. Quinn's English class on Monday morning, listening to Marnie answer a question about *The Miracle Worker,* she wished that she could be as blind and deaf as Helen Keller between 10 and 11 A.M. every school day. Then she wouldn't have to endure any more Marnie exposure. (It was bad enough that Nola had had that awkward stare-down with her ex-best friend at Stewart's on a *weekend.*)

Today Marnie strolled into class, looking as though she didn't have a care in the world, and turned her back to Nola with so much ease that it didn't even look deliberate anymore. A few days ago, this would have sent Nola reeling. But for some reason, Nola just calmly gazed out the window and got lost in her thoughts about everything that had happened to her in the last week — the "he loves me, he loves me not" drama with Matt, meeting Ian, seeing Riley's MySpace page.

Surprisingly, she'd made it through without any help from Marnie.

A little flutter of accomplishment rose into Nola's chest. *Maybe I don't need her after all.*

"Ladies and gentlemen, as you all know, group projects are upon us." Nola's eyes darted to the front of the room when Mr. Quinn spoke. "Usually, I let my students choose their own groups, but I find that one friend ends up pulling his or her weight and the others do the bare minimum. It's an unfair and uncomfortable situation for everyone involved."

*He doesn't know what unfair and uncomfortable really means*, Nola thought.

"My solution is to divide the groups up via the seating chart." Mr. Quinn took the cap off his marker and began writing on the dry-erase board. "So you'll be working with whoever is sitting diagonally from you."

*Did he just say,* diagonally?!?!

Nola shook her head. She had to have heard him wrong. Pairing her up with Marnie just as she was starting to feel a little better and stronger could be disastrous.

But when Mr. Quinn wrote these names in a column labeled Group 2 — Sally Applebaum, Marnie Fitzpatrick, Nola James, and Evan Sanders — Nola realized that this was absolutely for real.

Suddenly, Marnie's hand sprang back up. "Excuse me, Mr. Quinn," she squawked.

Mr. Quinn turned around and grinned. "Yes, Marnie?"

"Is there any way to . . . switch groups?" Marnie asked.

Nola felt her face become scalding hot. Why should

Marnie be the one asking to switch? Nola was the one who'd been made a fool of and irrevocably hurt! *She* should be asking Mr. Quinn to be reassigned, not Marnie.

"That's okay, Mr. Quinn. *I'll* switch," Nola said forcefully.

Mr. Quinn clasped his hands behind his back and leaned on his heels. "Well, obviously we have some sort of conflict here."

Nola sighed in relief. Mr. Quinn was about to become her most favorite teacher in the Poughkeepsie School District.

"However . . ."

*Oh, no! Not "however." Anything but "however"!*

"I think you both should look to Helen Keller as an example of how to triumph in the face of adversity," Mr. Quinn said before spinning back around to finish writing his list.

Nola leaned forward so her head hit the top of her desk. But it didn't have the desired effect of rendering her unconscious. Mr. Quinn had moved on to his next phase of torture — instructing them all to get into their groups and decide on their oral presentation topic.

Nola watched as Marnie got up and sat in an empty seat next to Sally. Then Evan passed by, grabbed a desk, and dragged it over to them. Nola was fuming at the idea of having to cooperate with her ex-best friend, but there wasn't another option. So Nola gathered all her things and wandered over to the desk in between Sally and Evan.

"So what do you guys think?" Sally enthused as Nola sheepishly took her seat. "Should we do our presentation on Anne Sullivan, or on the social impact of Braille?"

Evan shrugged his shoulders. "Either is fine with me."

"What about you, Nola?" Sally started making a tally in her notebook.

"Um, I think Braille might be a good topic," Nola replied as she looked straight at Marnie, who was bowing her head and picking at her fingernails. Nola still couldn't believe how good Marnie was at pretending she wasn't even there. The girl was unbelievable.

"Great." Sally bit her lip as she continued to scribble. "Marnie, do you like the Braille idea, too?"

Marnie elevated her eyes so that she caught Nola's gaze and then her brow furrowed. "Actually, Anne Sullivan's life is very interesting, and it's more directly related to the play."

Nola scowled. Marnie was just disagreeing because she wanted to piss off Nola. "But we could bring in Braille books and let everyone take a look at them," Nola countered.

"Visual aids are always cool," Evan muttered.

Nola flashed him a half-grin. It felt good to have somebody on her side.

"We could also teach the class Anne Sullivan's sign language technique. That's more useful, if you ask me," Marnie said, straightening up in her seat so that her chest stuck out.

Nola rolled her eyes. "What*ever*," she mumbled.

"Is there a problem, *Nola*?" Marnie snapped.

This was the first thing Marnie had said to Nola in a week, and the tone of it was just as mean, if not meaner, than the last thing Marnie had said to her. Nola just couldn't keep her anger in check.

"Um, yeah. *You* are my problem," she barked.

"What did I do now?" Marnie said snidely.

Nola felt an itch crawling up the back of her knees, but she tried not to think about it. "You're just going against the Braille idea because *I'm* for it!"

"Oh, *please*," Marnie said, chuckling.

If Marnie had said something vile, Nola probably would have been able to stomach it. But the fact that Marnie had just laughed in her face, as a nervous Sally and a perplexed Evan looked on, sent Nola into a downward spiral that no teeny bit of self-assuredness could stop.

The last thing Nola wanted was for Marnie to see

how much she took her actions to heart, so she got up and asked Mr. Quinn for a hall pass. Once Nola was outside the room, tears began streaming down her cheeks. As she approached the girls' bathroom, Nola saw two boys running down the corridor. Nola didn't realize who they were until they were a few feet away from her, and one of them in particular slowed down once he recognized Nola.

"Go ahead, Tucker. I'll catch up," Dane Harris said as he stopped and tried to catch his breath.

Nola wiped at her eyes quickly as Tucker dashed right by and hollered, "Later, bro!" Then she glanced at the girls' bathroom door.

*Just ten more steps.*

"We meet again, Mrs. Billingsworth," Dane said with a devilish grin.

Nola hadn't seen that smile since Marnie's god-awful birthday party. She instantly felt self-conscious so she crossed her arms in front of herself. "What do you want?"

"Do I have to want something in order to talk to you?" Dane pushed up the sleeves of his crewneck sweater one at a time, as if he were preparing to get his hands dirty.

"I can't think of another reason why you would," Nola said, remembering just how arrogant and rude

Dane had been on the deck of Lizette's lake house. She still had no idea what Marnie saw in him. Sure, everyone thought Dane was the perfect preppy guy, but couldn't Marnie see when she was up real close that he was just a creep in khaki pants?

"Wow, you're pretty cheeky for a maid." Dane raised his eyebrows. "I should really teach you some discipline. It's for your own good."

Dane had cornered Nola at quite an inopportune time, just like he had a couple of weeks ago. She was so upset that there was no *way* she was going to let Dane treat her like crap for his amusement's sake.

"Back up, preptard!" she shouted, poking him hard in the ribs. "Or you're going see how cheeky I *really* am!"

Nola stormed off to the bathroom before she could see the look on Dane's face. However, she did hear him yell, "You're gorgeous when you're angry, Mrs. B!" as the door closed behind her.

It was then that Nola realized why Marnie Fitzpatrick was enthralled by Dane Harris.

They both thought two faces were better than one.

# Chapter 17

Marnie loved getting manicures and pedicures at the Marlene Weber Day Spa. Not only was it a great place to unwind, but Mrs. Fitzpatrick was best friends with one of the managers, so Marnie, Erin, and their mom received sweet discounts on everything from nail polish and seaweed facials to eyebrow threading and thirty-minute massages.

After a long Monday at school, which had included that *über*-irritating face-off with Nola during English class, Marnie desperately needed some pampering. So she invited Lizette to come with her and partake in a two hour glamour-thon, complete with a reflexology session.

Sure, Marnie knew that Lizette's Mondays were reserved for "quality time" with Brynne, but Marnie felt that invading Brynne's turf was more than justified. Brynne had done nothing but bug the living hell out of Marnie this week. First, she'd baited Lizette and Grier into a New York City shopping spree on the same day of Marnie's important student council meeting, and then she conveniently left Marnie out of *Beauty and the Geek* viewing on Sunday. If she didn't retaliate now, Marnie would essentially be condoning Brynne's bratty behavior, and she wasn't about to let that happen.

Besides, Marnie had wanted to spend some alone time with Lizette so she could find out more about what happened between Lizette and Dane in the cab after Tucker's party. This missing earring story sounded extremely suspicious, especially because when Marnie had asked Dane about it, he'd said he couldn't remember much of what happened on the ride home. Marnie had watched enough of Kyra Sedgwick on *The Closer* to know that "I don't remember" was another way of saying "I'm hiding something."

As Marnie sat next to Lizette in neighboring pedicure lounge chairs, soaking their feet in pools of aromatic, bubbling, sudsy water, she felt a wave of anxiety rise into her chest. If something was going on with Lizette and Dane, what would Marnie do about it? Stop being friends with Lizette? Break up with Dane? Neither of those things even seemed like an option.

"Omigod, can you believe the dress that Fergie wore to the American Music Awards?" Lizette shoved an open copy of *People* magazine under Marnie's nose and made a disgusted face. "That is seriously *fugly*."

Marnie quickly assessed Lizette's attire for today — a pair of hot pink cropped sweatpants with a red-and-blue plaid Western snap front shirt tied up above the waist. On Fergie, this ensemble would have looked like a gigantic fashion misstep, but on Lizette, it looked absolutely glorious. No surprise there.

"If you could look like any celebrity, who would it be?" Marnie said through a couple of giggles. The nail technician was running a sloughing stone on the heel of her foot, and it really tickled.

"Sienna Miller," Lizette replied without hesitation. "She is, like, the empress of fierceness. Don't you think?"

"Yeah, she's super-pretty. But you know what, Zee? You already do look like her." Marnie knew that paying Lizette compliments like these weren't going to help her find out anything about Dane, but she figured it couldn't hurt to remind Lizette about what a good friend she was.

"Really?" Lizette's eyes brightened as she smiled.

"Definitely. Even Sawyer said something like that at Tucker's party," Marnie announced while rerolling the cuffs of her black Lucky jeans past her knees. She'd hoped that this comment would steer the conversation to the mystery cab ride, but after Marnie had said it, she couldn't get images of Sawyer at the Chinese restaurant out of her mind. It was so weird — one minute she was worried about her wonderful sorta boyfriend Dane and her good friend Lizette slinking off together, and the next she was fantasizing about Sawyer's perfect cheekbones. How was that even possible?

Lizette's grin morphed into a sour frown. Then she started flipping through her magazine, whipping each page so hard, Marnie was surprised that Lizette hadn't given herself a flesh wound. "Whatever, Sawyer is totally whack," she huffed.

"What do you mean?"

"He hasn't talked to me since Friday night." Lizette leaned over to inspect the technician's progress on her toes and then flopped back in her chair. She picked up the remote control and chose a massage setting. "Oh, did you ask Dane if he found my earring?"

"Yes, but he didn't have it," Marnie said, swallowing hard. "Actually, he doesn't remember much about the trip home."

Lizette snickered. "Well, there's not much to remember. He passed out cold."

"He did?"

"Yeah, like, the second the taxi driver pulled away from the curb." Lizette's voice was wobbly from the chair's vibrations. "I didn't notice I was missing an earring until I was getting ready for bed. I had both of them on when I left Tucker's, which is why I thought it must have come off in the cab."

*So nothing happened.* Marnie breathed a deep sigh of relief.

"Sorry, Zee," she said, patting her friend on the shoulder.

"I'm just *so* annoyed," Lizette moaned. "Sawyer was *all over me* at the luau and now he's freezing me out. It doesn't make any sense."

"Well, maybe he's been busy." Marnie knew this was a lame thing to say, especially because she had seen Sawyer on Sunday.

"Busy my ass." Lizette flipped another page in *People* magazine and then angrily tossed it aside. "He's probably scamming on somebody else."

"Don't be ridiculous. You said it yourself. He was all over you a few days ago." Marnie felt a little queasy when she thought of Sawyer pawing at Lizette, just as she had before when she'd pictured the same scenario with Dane.

*God, what is the matter with me?*

Then something bizarre happened. Lizette's lower lip started quivering. "Actually, Marn, *I* was all over *him*. He probably thinks I'm a skeezer. I shouldn't have had so much party punch."

Marnie was floored. Underneath the funky clothes and the smexy swagger, Lizette Levin was just as insecure as any other freshman girl at Poughkeepsie Central. In fact, Lizette probably took Sawyer's indifference much harder because she always got guys so easily. Other people would kill to have Lizette's problems, but still, Marnie was sympathetic.

"Honestly, I'm sure Sawyer is going to call you soon," Marnie said, sounding like the authority on boys, which she secretly enjoyed. "He's most likely following that stupid three-day rule so you don't think he's desperate."

Lizette examined her feet as the technician applied the topcoat. "I still think he likes someone else."

"Why do you keep saying that?" Marnie peered down at her feet, too. The shade of red she chose was coming out way darker than she thought it would. Instead of looking like rubies, her toenails looked like candied apples.

"Because," Lizette whined. "At the party, he kept disappearing every few minutes. He must have been talking to some other girl. Did you happen to see anything?"

Marnie thought back to Friday night. She remembered that Sawyer had come up and talked to her a few times. But other than that, Marnie hadn't seen anything out of the ordinary.

"Maybe you're being just a teensy bit paranoid, Zee," Marnie said, patting Lizette on the leg.

The sound of a Kelly Clarkson ring tone startled them both.

"That's me!" Lizette said excitedly. It was pretty obvious to Marnie that Lizette was hoping Sawyer was calling. Lizette looked at the caller ID and then frowned as she flipped open her phone. "Whaddya want, Brynne?"

Marnie rolled her eyes. *Here we go.*

"I'm at the day spa with Marnie, okay? God, be a professional stalker, why don't you?" Lizette snapped her phone shut. "Sorry about that. What were we talking about again?"

Marnie snickered. Lizette was just too much. "You wanted to know if I saw Sawyer talking with any girls at Tucker's party," she replied.

"Ugh, right," Lizette muttered. "Are you sure you didn't see anything?"

Marnie was about to reassure Lizette when she got such a chill she thought someone had just jacked up the air-conditioning. If Marnie told Lizette that she and Sawyer were hanging out at the party, would Lizette get all suspicious? From the way she was talking, Lizette was convinced that something bad was up.

The last thing Marnie wanted to do was worry her friend needlessly.

So instead of answering, Marnie leaned over, took her hand, and splashed some water from her basin onto Lizette, sending them into a laughing fit that lasted until they got their manicures.

# Chapter 18

"Who wants Chex Party Mix?" Matt asked while walking into his living room and holding out an enormous Tupperware bowl filled to the brim with the wholesome yet salty snack.

Nola put down her KISS pencil and rubbed her hands together in anticipation. It was 7 P.M. on Tuesday night. Nola, Matt, Iris, and Evan had been studying together for more than an hour now, so she definitely had a severe case of the cramming munchies.

"Well, aren't you the spitting image of Martha Stewart," Iris said, slamming her math textbook shut and leaping up from the couch. She sprinted over to Matt and tried to put her hand in the bowl, but Matt jerked it away.

"Don't you think I look more like Rachael Ray?" he joked.

Evan was sitting on the floor and crouching over the coffee table when he looked up from his graph paper and smirked. "Totally. She's the hottest chef on the Food Network."

Matt walked toward Evan and held the bowl out to him. "Thanks, man. Chex your brains out."

Evan grabbed a handful of mix and shoved it in his mouth. Nola giggled when Evan didn't seem to notice all the crumbs on his "Future Trophy Husband" T-shirt. "Wow, this stuff is awesome."

Matt made his way over to Nola, who was seated in the black leather La-Z-Boy recliner in the corner of the room. "I got the recipe from my new best friend," he said, offering the bowl to Nola and winking at her.

Nola grinned as she pushed up the sleeves on her gray fleece Columbia pullover and took a small handful of mix. Matt had been acting especially nice to Nola since her spat with Marnie in English yesterday. In fact, he had arranged this after-school study group because he wanted to give Nola the opportunity to socialize with her new circle of friends, or so he'd said.

Still, Nola had pretty much kept to herself this evening, speaking only when someone asked her a question. Instead of taking notes on Act Two of *The Miracle Worker*, Nola had slyly written *Matthew Thomas Heatherly* over and over again on the back cover of her notebook, as if doing so would make him want to whisk Nola off to some secluded cabin in the wilderness and kiss her until the sun rose from behind the Adirondack Mountains. Unfortunately, the only thing that came of it was a bad cramp in Nola's right hand.

Matt approached Iris once again, clutching the bowl to his chest. Iris tried to scoop up some mix, but Matt moved away before she could get any.

"Give me the bowl, or you'll lose an eye," Iris demanded with a ferocious glare.

Matt laughed as he felt one of his front pockets with his right hand. "Iris, you've been saved by the bell." He gave Iris the bowl, and she retreated to the couch in victory. Then Matt reached into his pocket and pulled out his cell phone.

Nola dug her nails into the arms of the recliner. She had seen the grin that just crawled across Matt's face several times before, and each time she had, she'd felt the exact same way — scalding-hot-under-the-collar jealous. Nola glanced down at all the *Matthew Thomas Heatherly*s she'd scribbled and asked herself how long she could subject herself to this anguish. Losing Marnie had been bad enough, but watching Matt fawn over some fabulous, smart, funny girl, who would be coming to visit him in four days, was almost worse.

"Hey, Rye," Matt said into the phone. He paced back and forth in front of the oak entertainment center, which needed to be cleaned with a Swiffer dust mop or two. "Of course, I'm excited about Saturday. I miss you so much."

Nola took her KISS pencil and began erasing like crazy.

"Are you kidding? There is plenty of stuff to do in Poughkeepsie." Matt flopped down on the couch next to Iris and stretched out so his Doc Martens–clad feet landed on Iris's lap. Iris tried to push him away, but Matt seemed hell-bent on annoying her. "I'm going to take you to all my favorite places. And I've told my dad everything there is to know about you, so he's real eager to impress my girlfriend with a fancy dinner. How does that sound?"

Nola was pushing so hard on her pencil eraser that she tore a hole in the cardboard.

"You are too sweet for words," Matt cooed while cradling the phone against his shoulder.

Suddenly, Iris poked Matt hard in the stomach. Just like Nola, she apparently had heard way more than she wanted to. "Get a room, lover boy. We're trying to expand our minds in here."

Evan echoed the sentiment by tossing some Chex Party Mix at Matt.

"Okay, okay. I'll take this upstairs," Matt said, getting up from the couch and covering the mouthpiece of the phone with his hand. "But if I come back and all the food is gone, I will be forced to arm wrestle every last one of you."

Evan kept tossing Chex at his target until Matt bounded out of the living room, which made Nola both chuckle and let out a tiny sigh of relief.

"You made a mess in here, Sanders," Iris said, gesturing to the pieces of Chex that had landed all over the shag carpet.

Evan stared at her blankly. "So?"

"Don't 'so' me. Go get a vacuum and clean it up," she barked.

"I don't even know where to find one," Evan replied in an aggravated voice.

"Then I suggest you sniff around here like a blood-hound until you do," Iris said coolly.

Evan growled as he got up and marched off in search of a high-powered Bissell.

Iris laughed and directed her gaze at Nola. "I can be *such* a bitch, huh?"

Nola was preoccupied with biting on her pencil and thinking about the cute things Matt was saying to Riley, so she just nodded her head.

"Let me guess," Iris said as she lay back on the couch, her navy blue ribbed turtleneck pulling up a little so Nola could see her navel. "You're crushing on Matt, aren't you?"

And now Iris had Nola's undivided attention.

"No, I'm not!" Nola said so emphatically that she practically ejected herself out of the La-Z-Boy.

Iris snickered. "Come on, Nola. It's written all over your face."

Nola put her palms on her cheeks, which felt very warm to the touch. "I'm just flushed, that's all."

"Well, you're 'flushed' every time Matt is within one hundred yards of you." Iris took a throw pillow and put it behind her neck. "How do you explain that?"

Nola opened her mouth with the intention of lying her butt off, but nothing came out. If truth be told, Nola's throat felt so scratchy and constricted, she wondered if a piece of Rice Chex was lodged in there. If there was, she hoped she'd choke on it any minute, because that would be better than admitting she frequently fantasized about kissing Matt Heatherly at the senior prom. Sure, it was four years away, but given how slow Nola operated, it seemed like quite the reasonable timetable.

"Your silence speaks volumes, girl," Iris teased. "But don't worry. Your secret is safe with me."

Nola reopened her notebook and hid behind it. She couldn't bear the thought of anyone seeing the embarrassed expression on her face, least of all Matt.

"One word of caution, though," Nola heard Iris say. "I've known Matt since fifth grade. He's a . . . complicated guy, with a lot of problems lurking beneath the surface."

Nola's stomach responded by gurgling loudly. *What type of problems does she mean? The get-suspended-from-school kind? The not-having-a-mother-around kind? What?!*

"Just be careful, okay? He's had his heart broken

a couple of times, and it really messed him up," Iris added. "Besides, he's smitten with that Riley chick. Unreciprocated love ain't where it's at. You feelin' me?"

Nola was feelin' Iris big-time, but before she could reply or ask for more details about Matt's so-called problems, he sauntered back into the room, grinning.

"I thought you were expanding your mind, Iris," he said, crossing his arms over his chest.

"I'm taking a breather," she said while closing her eyes.

Matt ambled over to Nola and kneeled down in front of her. "Hey, I need to ask a favor," he whispered.

Nola remembered what Iris said about her face getting flushed whenever Matt was near and suddenly it was hard for her to breathe. "Okay," she said softly.

"I want to give Riley a 'Welcome to Poughkeepsie' present."

*Gag.*

"And I was hoping you could help me out."

*Gag. Gag.*

"Would you mind making her a necklace or something?"

*Okay, I think I just threw up in my mouth a little.*

"She just loves handmade jewelry, and honestly, yours is the best I've seen. It would really mean a lot to me."

Nola felt a sharp stabbing pain in her stomach.

Under no circumstances was this proposal a good idea. How could she possibly make Riley *anything*? Not only would Nola be forced into a perpetual state of hives, but her precious craft would be forever contaminated by this heinous act. She had to say no. There was no other solution. Matt would have to give his super-cool girl-friend something else.

Nola inhaled deeply and then spit out "I don't know" when she exhaled.

It wasn't quite the "hell no, sucker!" she had planned on saying, but perhaps it would still do the job.

"Well, I'd be willing to pay for the supplies and labor," Matt suggested. "You name the price. Whatever you think is fair."

*Oh, god, he's actually negotiating with me.*

"It's not that," Nola replied.

"Then what is it?"

As Nola stared into Matt's dreamy hazel eyes and gazed at his thin, yet nibble-worthy lips, all of her defenses shut down. She wasn't able to come up with any kind of excuse not to say yes, and although she still knew what a disaster this could turn out to be, the bottom line was this: Nola didn't want to let Matt down.

"Nothing," Nola said, bringing her notebook close to the gaping hole in her heart. "I'm happy to do it."

*For you. Just you.*

# Chapter 19

*Prep Work for Tomorrow: A Must Memorize List*

1.  Go over every syllable of my speech with Dane tonight until I can recite it flawlessly. (Special note to self: Do this over the phone so you're not distracted by his scorching hotness and wandering/most excellent hands.)
2.  Practice the visualization techniques Zee gave me, especially the one where I imagine the student body throwing rose petals at my feet as I'm crowned freshman class treasurer. It's silly, but who cares? Maybe it'll work!
3.  Line up possible outfits and make a final decision already!
4.  DO NOT think about a certain person of the male persuasion whose first name rhymes with lawyer.
5.  PUT ON YOUR GAME FACE! UH-HUH! THAT'S RIGHT!

After having a nice, quiet Wednesday night shish kebab dinner with her mom, Marnie holed up in her room for almost an hour, rehearsing her speech for the following day's assembly while Dane listened on the phone. Even though Marnie had spent a lot of hours writing up flash cards and hanging posters in recent days, she wasn't feeling as confident as she should about her chances of winning. Lizette had been a fine campaign manager, but Marnie was all too aware of how much time she and Lizette had been spending at the Galleria or hanging out at the grandiose Levin sprawl when they had intended on planning a strategy that would level Jeremy Atwood and anyone else who stood in their way of total treasury domination.

However, Lizette seemed confident enough for the both of them. This morning, she'd canvassed the entire freshman class to see who everyone was voting for. Marnie had come out so far on top that Lizette had joked that Marnie didn't even need to bother showing up for the assembly. She was that much of a sure thing.

Still, Marnie was determined to deliver a fantastic speech tomorrow, regardless of her sneaking suspicion that her fellow students were supporting the Fitzpatrick campaign in part because of Lizette's popularity. She kept telling herself that once she approached the podium, everyone would be looking at *her* — not Lizette or Dane or Erin or anyone else she was somehow attached to. And whatever came out of Marnie's mouth would be etched into the audience's collective consciousness forever. Or at least until homecoming, which was about three or so weeks from now.

Either way, her high school persona was riding on this speech, and Marnie had to get it right or die a slasher-flick type death trying.

"So do you think I should mention that I spent one year as a Girl Scout?" Marnie was spinning around in her desk chair and playing with the cord of her cell's hands-free earpiece.

The sound of Dane's laugh made Marnie melt. "*Please* tell me you kept the uniform."

"Oh, my god, you did *not* just say that."

"I did indeed. I could go one step further and insist on *ordering some cookies*," he said slyly.

This had been going on for twenty minutes. Every time Marnie asked Dane a question about her speech, he would turn her words around and make some kind of sexy joke out of them. Marnie thought it was cute, and exciting, too. But it wasn't helping Marnie calm her slight public-speaking jitters. Sure, Dane was used to addressing the entire school, but how could he expect Marnie to be so flippant when so much was on the line?

"Come on, Dane. I really need to focus," Marnie coaxed.

"Fine, ruin my fun," Dane muttered.

"I'm sorry. I just want everything to be perfect."

Marnie stopped spinning, got up, and wobbled over to her bed. She laid down on her back and tied her yellow terrycloth robe around her tightly. Her mom always waited until the last possible minute to turn on the heat in the house, even if that meant struggling through a few freezing autumn and early winter nights.

"You're worrying too much," Dane replied. "People *like* you, Marnie, and I doubt anyone would notice if you messed up a little."

Marnie smiled at Dane's comforting words. "Well, that's easy for you to say. You're definitely going to get reelected, Mr. V.P."

Dane chuckled. "I hope so. Being in student council has a ton of perks that I would never want to give up."

"Like what?"

"Um . . . like getting invited to all the Majors parties and making out with the most unbelievably gorgeous soon-to-be freshman class treasurer in Poughkeepsie Central's illustrious history."

"Wow, you are laying it on pretty thick," Marnie said through a series of giggles as she kicked off her fuzzy white slippers onto the floor.

"Sorry, babe. I just can't control myself when I'm talking to you." Dane's voice was so smooth and silky that Marnie wanted to wrap herself in it for days on end.

"Is that so?" Marnie imagined what she and Dane would be doing if he was in her room right now — snuggling next to each other, she kissing his yummy neck while he ran his big, strong hands down the back of her cotton T-shirt. Suddenly, Marnie felt light-headed.

"Maybe I should come over and show you," Dane said breathily.

"Well, I — um," Marnie stammered. How was she supposed to respond to *that*?

Thankfully, the call-waiting beeped, giving Marnie a quick out.

"Hold on a sec, someone's on the other line," she said.

"I'm not going anywhere," Dane replied.

Marnie hit the FLASH button and swapped her calls. "Hello?"

The loud background noise, which sounded just like a college party, tipped Marnie off immediately.

*Erin.*

"CAN YOU HEAR ME?!" her sister shouted into the phone.

Marnie stuck a finger in her left ear. "Barely. Where are you?"

"IT'S MARDI GRAS IN HAPPY VALLEY! WHEEEE!!!"

Marnie rolled her eyes. This was the first of many sisterly drunk dials yet to come, she was sure of that. "Mardi Gras doesn't happen until February, Erin."

"WHAT?!" Erin screamed.

"WHY ARE YOU CALLING?" Marnie yelled back.

*God, it's like talking to freaking Grams the Gym teacher.*

Erin gurgled a bit before shouting again. "MOM TOLD ME TO WISH YOU LUCK FOR TOMORROW."

Marnie grinned. Maybe her sister wasn't so self-absorbed.

"SO DON'T MESS UP! THE LAST THING I WANT TO HEAR ABOUT WHEN I COME BACK FOR HOMECOMING IS THAT YOUR SPEECH SUCKED!"

Scratch that. *Self-absorbed* wasn't quite the right adjective to describe Erin Fitzpatrick.

Marnie hit the FLASH button again without saying anything else. She'd rather get back to Dane and their sexy conversation. However, when she looked at her phone she noticed that Dane had already hung up.

*That's weird.*

Marnie dialed Dane's number, but after the phone rang five times, it went straight to voice mail. Marnie cleared her throat before leaving a message.

"Hey, Dane, um, I guess our call got dropped or something. Anyway, call me back when you can, okay? Bye."

Marnie tossed her phone onto her bed and started rereading all of her flash cards as if nothing was wrong. But when she turned the lights off and pulled the covers up to her chin, Marnie wondered why her phone hadn't rung once the rest of night.

# Chapter 20

That same evening, Nola was trying to organize her jewelry-making supplies on the living-room window seat while Dennis and Dylan played a game, where they'd put each other in headlocks until one or the other cried out, "Mercy!" Currently, Dennis was in the lead. Or was it Dylan? Nola usually lost track after ten mercies, so who really knew.

"Come on, *say it*!" Dennis shouted as he wrangled Dylan onto the couch.

"No! You can't make me!" Dylan yelled back, his face turning pink.

When Nola looked up, she could see Dennis putting the pressure on. "Oh, yes, I can," he growled and yanked Dylan backward. Unfortunately, the boys lost their footing and fell into Nola's cluster of open Gladware, knocking beads and stones and clasps into a jumbled mess on the floor.

As soon as Dennis saw the rage in Nola's eyes, he muttered, "Oops," and dashed out of the room with Dylan trailing behind him.

Nola was at her wit's end. Not only did she have to endure the endless torment of doing a sick, twisted favor for the guy she was secretly in love with, but she also had to put up with the crazy antics of her brothers, who were obviously possessed by demons.

What made matters even worse was that the college boy her parents had hired to watch the twerps was utterly incompetent. Ian Capshaw couldn't control the kids any better than Nola could (which she thought was rather pathetic), had a bad attitude, and an even worse habit of being extremely nosy and annoying, and if the clamoring in the kitchen was any kind of hint, he couldn't cook, either.

After taking a few cleansing breaths, Nola stepped over the gigantic heap of tiny beads and glossy stones that had formed on the floor. She stalked to the laundry room with the intention of grabbing a broom and dustpan, but when she heard Ian yell out in pain, she bolted into the kitchen.

Nola got there just in time to see Ian hopping around and frantically waving his right hand in the air. He looked so ridiculous that she couldn't stop herself from laughing.

But Ian wasn't amused. He lunged at the sink and turned on the faucet, then held his right hand under the running water. "Oh, yeah, third-degree burns are *so freaking hilarious!*" he snapped.

Nola managed to quell her laughter and put on a straight face. "Are you okay?"

Ian rolled his eyes as droplets of water sprayed all over his ribbed burgundy zip-up sweater. "I'm phenomenal, thanks for asking."

"What happened?" Nola approached Ian slowly and when she was in close range, she leaned over his shoulder so she could see if he was badly hurt. His skin was a tad red, but luckily it didn't look too bad.

"I was boiling some tortellini and the side of my hand brushed up against the pot," Ian explained through a few painful winces.

"You know, ice works better." Nola walked over to the refrigerator, opened the freezer, and pulled out the coldest of Dr. James's emergency cold packs.

Ian shook his head and his well-combed hair became tousled in a particular way that reminded Nola of Matt. "I don't need one of those. I'm fine."

*So much for being anything like Matt. This guy is just as bad as Dane, if not more of a jerk!*

"Whatever you say." She threw the cold pack in the freezer and slammed the door shut.

"Everything is under control in here, so you can go back to weaving friendship bracelets or whatever it was you were doing," Ian mocked her.

Nola was in no mood for his taunting, but at the same time, she didn't feel like putting up much of a fight. Storming out of the kitchen and locking herself in her bedroom seemed like a good compromise. Nola was about to turn on her heel and march away, but she heard a sizzling sound coming from the stove. Her eyes darted in that direction and she saw the pot bubbling over because the top was still on.

Ian craned his neck so he could witness the disaster. "Oh, no!" he shouted.

Nola would have raced over and helped College Boy — she *really* would have — if he hadn't insulted her a moment ago. Instead, she just stood there with her arms crossed in front of her chest and a smirk on her face.

Ian dashed over to the island counter to snatch a blue dish towel. As the pot continued to spew hot water, he tried to gingerly pick up the top with the towel in his left hand, but so much steam was billowing out that he clearly couldn't see what he was doing.

The longer this went on, the more worried Nola became. Standing idly by in order to make the point that Ian was a total loser didn't seem as important as making sure the house didn't burn down. Nola dashed into the laundry room and grabbed a mop. When she got back to the kitchen, Ian had turned off the burner and was trying to fan the steam away as a puddle of water formed at his feet.

"Here, let me help —"

"Nola, look out!"

But the warning came too late. Nola slipped on the wet floor, her legs flew out from under her, and she landed right on her butt. Suddenly, Nola and Ian were in such hysterics that tears were streaming down their cheeks and they were barely able to speak.

"I-I'm s-sorry," Ian stammered as he tried to catch his breath.

Nola wiped at her eyes. "M-me, too."

Ian held out his uninjured hand and Nola grabbed ahold of it. He gently pulled her up so that she was staring directly into his face. She hadn't noticed before that Ian had a tiny scar on his chin, or that there was a small bump on the bridge of his nose, or that the shape of his eyebrows was practically flawless.

"You're not catching me at my best, believe me," Ian said, loosening his grip so that Nola could easily slip away. "Your brothers are crushing my soul."

"I can relate to that," Nola replied.

"I doubt I'm catching you in your prime, either," Ian said.

"What do you mean?"

Ian smiled deviously. "Well, most girls your age aren't in their pajamas by seven o'clock."

Nola looked down at her outfit — which consisted

of black athletic pants with white stripes on the sides and a gray Fila T-shirt — and then back up at Ian. "I wore this *to school*."

"Oh," Ian said as he tried to cover up his widening grin with his injured hand. "I just thought — forget it."

"Forget what?" Nola asked defensively.

Ian sighed in frustration. "I just thought you were depressed, that's all."

"Because of how I'm *dressed*?" Nola was completely caught off guard. Even though she did feel kind of depressed, who did Ian think he was, Captain of the Happy Mood Patrol? Where did he get off saying this stuff when he didn't even know her?

"Well, you have the traditional 'I've been dumped' uniform on, complete with messy ponytail. What else was I supposed to think?"

In an instant, Nola realized that she *had* been dumped, not only by her best friend, but by a guy who she wasn't even dating. How lame was that?

Still, did this stuck-up, pompous Vassar student need to point it out? Hell no!

Getting in Ian's face didn't seem like a big deal at this point. In fact, Nola really had nothing to lose, not even her pride — Ian had already labeled her an undatable slob based on her choice in loungewear and her low-maintenance hairstyle.

"I don't know, Ian. Maybe you should rethink your course list and *learn how to boil freaking water*," she said snarkily.

The tiny surge of satisfaction Nola got when she saw the stunned look Ian's face vanished as she walked back into the living room and saw her supplies scattered all over the floor. Suddenly, it dawned on her that she had only three days to pull together Riley's "Welcome to Poughkeepsie" present. Three days until Riley was staying in Matt's house while Mr. Heatherly played a gig in Manhattan and Mrs. Heatherly was nowhere to be found.

But what bothered Nola even more than Riley's impending visit was how someone like Ian had been able to see right through her . . . just like someone else used to.

# Chapter 21

On Thursday morning, Marnie sprang out of her bed before there was any light outside. Her alarm wasn't supposed to go off for another hour and a half, but her internal clock won the battle of wills. Actually, Marnie was a big believer in the mind-body connection, so when her eyes snapped open at 5 A.M., she didn't try to fight it. Obviously, her body knew that her mind was under a lot of stress and that today a nice long run was an absolute must.

Marnie yanked off her cami and boxer short sleep set and slipped on her sports bra, a loose fitting T-shirt, and a pair of Adidas breakaway track pants. This work-out ensemble made Marnie feel badass and competitive, which was exactly how she wanted to feel when she gave her speech this afternoon at the assembly. When she laced up her gray-and-orange New Balance cross-trainers, Marnie felt a surge of adrenaline.

Marnie padded down the stairs quietly so she wouldn't wake her mom and grabbed her windbreaker out of the hall closet. She did a few light stretches on the lawn and even broke out the two yoga poses that she'd "mastered" after one session.

Once Marnie started down her jogging route, every

thought in her head immediately came into stark focus. Typically, this kind of mental clarity didn't hit her until after she'd finished her first mile, but for some reason, it kicked in a lot sooner today.

As visions of Dane, Lizette, Jeremy, Nola, and the election danced in her head, Marnie sprinted as fast as she could down the cracked and uneven pavement. Her calves were burning with each step, and her heart was thumping so rapidly that Marnie was afraid she might collapse in the middle of the crosswalk. And from the looks of the elderly crossing guard standing on the corner, her chances of survival seemed as slim as one of those skinny doctors on *Grey's Anatomy*.

Marnie slowed down when her sides began to ache and stopped the moment she started to feel nauseous. She bent over and put her hands on her knees, her head hanging down, and moisture dampening the back of her neck.

*Okay, easy does it.*

She regulated her breathing until it steadied and closed her eyes as she concentrated on standing up straight. But when she opened her eyes and saw she had somehow ended up in front of Nola's beautiful Victorian house, Marnie gasped.

The sun was coming up and casting shadows onto the porch. Last summer, Marnie and Nola would sit there all day, talking and listening to Nola's i-deck, which was blasting through her bedroom window. When the sound of Nola's laugh echoed in Marnie's ear, the pinch in her stomach became much harder to ignore.

*It's just a bad cramp. It'll pass,* she tried to convince herself.

However, whatever it was kept hold of Marnie as she limped all the way home and until Mr. Levin's luxurious SUV came to pick her up for school an hour later.

"Oh. My. God. You. Look. FABULOUS!" Lizette squealed when Marnie crawled into the back of Mr. Levin's Mercedes.

"You really think so?" Marnie glanced down and did a quick inventory of her outfit, which had come yesterday afternoon, courtesy of bluefly.com, her mom's Visa card, and Express Mail: a black cotton Betsey Johnson pin-tuck miniskirt, a purple kimono style sweater, and a pair of dark brown suede knee-high wedge boots engineered by designer Charles David, topped off with her favorite vintage jean jacket.

"There is no way in hell anyone will vote for that Jeremy dork when they get a look at you," Lizette said as she adjusted her seat belt so it wasn't crushing the huge fabric flower that she'd pinned to her vintage, sky-blue puffy-sleeved secretary shirt.

"Well, I owe it all to my amazing campaign manager," Marnie said, winking and nudging Lizette with her elbow.

"Yeah, ya do!" Lizette fished out her compact from her oversize tan Marc Jacobs bag and blotted her nose. She turned and dabbed Marnie's chin with some powder, then grinned. "So, are you nervous?"

*Nervous enough that I threw up in the shower!*

"Not really," Marnie lied. "Dane and I went over my speech last night so —"

Lizette interrupted her with loud kissing noises and a few obscene gestures.

Marnie rolled her eyes. "Will you stop?"

"Just admit it, Marn. You want to get with Vice President Harris in *an undisclosed location!*" Lizette joked.

Marnie laughed so hard that Mr. Levin looked in the rearview mirror to see what all the fuss was about. When Lizette started in with more state-of-the-art sound effects, the both of them began cracking up. Marnie was so happy to be hanging out with Lizette right now. She knew just how to take Marnie's mind off everything, and given how cluttered her mind was earlier, that was no small feat.

Ten minutes later, Marnie and Lizette piled out of the car and waved good-bye to Mr. Levin. As they walked up the pathway toward the foreboding facade of Poughkeepsie Central High School, Marnie could feel that sharp pinching sensation in her stomach again. It was most likely just nerves. Still, she couldn't help but consider the possibility that her appendix was about to rupture. That would really put a damper on her speech.

Luckily, Lizette was quick to point out how many people were rubbernecking as Marnie strode by, looking every bit the part of a freshman class treasurer. "I'm telling you, it's going to be a landslide," Lizette whispered as they approached the front doors.

Marnie felt uneasy, though. People were definitely gawking at her, but not in the admiring way that they had at Tucker's luau. In fact, it was the exact opposite. Marnie's classmates were snickering and flashing obnoxious smirks when they looked at her. Something was definitely wrong.

When they strolled into the hallway, even Lizette picked up on the strange, menacing laughter that surrounded them. The pain in Marnie's stomach intensified as she rushed through the crowd toward her locker — but the sight of one of her posters stopped her cold.

Someone had written a few words on it in bold purple marker.

Marnie sprinted a few feet down the hall and saw

that another one of her signs had the same thing scribbled all over it.

She didn't have to run throughout the school to know that every one of them had been vandalized. But what made matters worse was the words that were scrawled next to Marnie's name.

### The Thong Thief

*Oh, my god, everything's ruined*, Marnie thought as she tried not to cry.

At first, Lizette's eyes were wide with horror, but then she got in touch with her angry side real quick. "Okay, which one of you cretins did this?" she shouted at the top of her lungs. When no one spoke up, Lizette grabbed Marnie's hand and led her down the hall.

But the getaway wasn't going to be easy. Two junior-class boys walked alongside Marnie and started singing that stupid old Sisqó song. "Let me see that thong! Thong-th-thong-thong-thong." Then a couple more boys joined in. Next, some girls got in on the act, followed by Marnie's favorite person, Brynne Callaway.

Lizette must have seen Marnie's lower lip quivering and eyes filling up with tears, because she grabbed Marnie by the hand and dragged her off into the bathroom. As Marnie composed herself in one of the stalls, Lizette went on a wild rant about who could have wrecked the posters, which helped Marnie turn her utter embarrassment into anger.

There was only one suspect, and once Marnie stepped foot into English class, she was going to eat Nola James for breakfast and then spit her out.

# Chapter 22

Nola hadn't faked being sick since the seventh grade, when she wanted to get out of doing the National Physical Fitness Test in gym class (she was a disaster at squat thrusts). But when she'd seen what happened to Marnie's posters this morning, Nola figured that Marnie would be waiting to strike during English class. As much as Nola hated her life at the moment, she definitely didn't want to risk losing it.

When Nola arrived at the school's infirmary, Mrs. Mulchahy, the school nurse, put a cold compress on Nola's head and had her lie down. Once Mrs. Mulchahy closed the door and turned off the light, the headache that Nola was only pretending to have turned into a real full-blown migraine. After all, Nola had come to the harsh realization that Matt had told someone else the secret he'd promised to take to his grave.

Nola didn't want to believe this, but what other explanation could there be? Prior to telling Matt about the Victoria's Secret debacle, Marnie was the *only person* who knew about it (not counting Mrs. Fitzpatrick). Maybe Matt let it slip by accident in front of Iris or Evan, or perhaps someone with a grudge against Marnie forced it out of him. But no matter how many scenarios she ran through her mind, it wouldn't change the fact that Marnie had been exposed as "The Thong Thief," and that the blame for this public relations fiasco would ultimately fall on Nola.

In a vain effort to calm her nerves, Nola sat up for a few minutes and rubbed her temples. It didn't help the pain at all, but at least it was keeping her occupied.

But then another distraction came in the form of a soft voice ringing out from behind the door.

"Hey, you okay?"

*Oh. God. No.*

Matt slipped into the room and sat down next to Nola. Seeing Matt for the first time on any given day usually brought Nola such happiness that she practically bounced up and down. But now there was just a sinking feeling in her chest that wouldn't disappear, regardless of the sincere smile on his adorable face or the way his scabbed knee poked out through the hole in his jeans.

"How did you know I was here?" Nola muttered.

"When you weren't in homeroom, I asked Ms. Lucas for a hall pass and took a wild guess." Matt chuckled.

But Nola was in no mood for Matt's jokes. This Thong Thief ordeal was *his* fault, and he was acting way too jovial for someone who was about to beg for her forgiveness. "So are you going to tell me what happened or what?" she asked.

"That's weird. I was going to ask you the same thing," Matt said confusedly.

Nola was aghast. Was Matt going to actually pretend that he wasn't responsible? Maybe Marnie had been right about him. "Um, Matt, let's get one thing straight. You're the one who blabbed, not me."

Matt looked completely stricken by Nola's accusation. "What are you talking about? I didn't say a word."

Nola rolled her eyes and then turned away from him.

"I'm telling the truth, Nola. I would never betray your trust like that," he urged.

*Yeah, where have I heard that before?*

"Look at me, Nola."

Nola couldn't help but cave when she heard just how upset Matt sounded. She turned back around and gazed into his cloudy hazel eyes.

"I swear I didn't talk smack about Marnie. Please believe me."

Nola really wanted to — she couldn't stand to lose someone else she was close to. But at the same time, she just couldn't bring herself to absolve Matt of any culpability without knowing how everything had played out.

All of a sudden, Mrs. Mulchahy stormed into the room with her broad shoulders, white jumper, and off-white tights. Even though it was quite dim, Nola could tell Mrs. Mulchahy was not happy to see Matt disturbing a sick patient.

"And what are you doing in here, Matthew?" Mrs. Mulchahy crossed her thick arms in front of her ample bosom and sneered.

Matt sprang to his feet. "Oh, I was just . . . looking for —"

"Good-bye, Mr. Heatherly," she said firmly.

Matt gave Mrs. Mulchahy a little bow and then darted out the door without even a glance in Nola's direction.

"Are you feeling any better, hon?" Mrs. Mulchahy rubbed Nola's shoulders gently. "Or would you like me to call your mom and have her pick you up and take you home?"

Nola wasn't feeling any better or worse than before. In fact, right now she felt numb. But the more she thought about how easy it was for Matt to make her ignore her gut instincts, the more she wanted to escape Poughkeepsie Central and the imminent wrath of Marnie Fitzpatrick. So she gave Mrs. Mulchahy her mom's cell phone number, then curled into a ball and waited.

Twenty minutes later, Nola's mom came and picked her up from school in the family's silver Subaru Forester. Dr. James was still wearing her white lab coat from Saint

IN **180** OUT

Francis Hospital and a stethoscope around her neck, which meant that she had left work in a hurry. As Nola sat silently and watched the neighborhood pass by through the passenger side window, she choked back tears. She just felt so overwhelmed with everything that was happening in her life, she couldn't keep it bottled up any longer.

"Nola, are you all right? Nurse Mulchahy said you had a migraine."

When Nola heard the genuine concern in her mom's voice, tears began to stream down her face. It wasn't long before Nola was sobbing uncontrollably.

"Nola? What's wrong, sweetie?" Dr. James said as she pulled the car over to the side of the road and put the gearshift in park. "Honey, I can't help you if you don't tell me what's bothering you."

Nola was crying over so many things, she didn't even know where to start. "I . . . it's . . . ," she stuttered.

Her mother ran her hands though Nola's hair. "Just take a deep breath and say the first thing that comes into your head."

Nola followed her mom's advice, breathing in through her nose and out through her mouth. "Marnie and I . . . we're not friends anymore," she mumbled.

Her mom appeared stricken. "What on earth happened?"

"It doesn't matter. She's friends with this other girl now," Nola said as she rubbed her eyes. "And she *hates* me."

"I'm sure she doesn't hate you, Nola." Her mother took her hand. "Sometimes people just grow apart. It's painful for a while, but then you'll make new friends and it won't hurt as much."

This only made Nola cry harder. "I *did* make a new friend."

"Well, that's great!" Her mom was trying really hard to be upbeat.

"No, it isn't," Nola wailed as she bowed her head. "I *like* him, but he has a girlfriend."

The awkward pause signaled to Nola that her mom was at a loss for words. She pulled her head back up and gazed at her mother through her blurry eyes.

Dr. James smiled and caressed Nola's cheek lovingly. Then she took her stethoscope, put the earbuds in, and held the cold plastic disk against Nola's chest. When she was done listening, her mom smirked and said, "I think this is a triple hot fudge sundae emergency. Does Stewart's sound okay?"

Nola looked at the clock on the dashboard, which read 9:45. "But Stewart's isn't even open yet."

Dr. James furrowed her brow. "Then we'll run to the store, buy some sundae-making supplies, and go home."

"But what about work?" Nola sniffled.

"I've got someone more important to care for," her mom said, grinning. "And sundaes to make."

Nola hugged her mom tightly. "Thank you."

"It would be my pleasure," her mom whispered into her ear, "if you'd let *me* be your best friend today."

Nola gave her mom an extra squeeze. Right now, there was nothing she could have wanted more.

# Chapter 23

At 2:10 P.M., every student from Poughkeepsie Central High School was crammed onto the auditorium bleachers for the big student council assembly. Those who were running for office were tucked away backstage, reading over their speeches one final time until the principal called them each by name to the podium. Except for Marnie, that is. She was much too busy worrying to even consider scanning her flash cards or practicing her smile.

All day long, Marnie had been in a state of panic. Not only did she have to endure constant staring, snickering, pointing, laughing, whispering, and, of course, singing, but she also had to suck it up and pretend like none of it bothered her. After spending a good forty-five minutes freaking out in the girls' bathroom, Marnie calmed down with the help of Lizette and realized that if she acted bent out of shape about what happened to her posters, then people would keep making a big deal out of it.

So far, Marnie hadn't crumbled in public once, thanks to Lizette's frequent encouraging text messages and a girl-power powwow during lunch. Still, as composed as Marnie seemed on the outside, she felt just as she had a couple of weeks ago when she and Nola had had their epic showdown.

Marnie clenched her fists at the thought of Nola defacing all of her posters and exposing that embarrassing secret of hers. Marnie was amazed that Nola could even do something this cruel. Although there didn't seem to be another suspect, Marnie had moments of doubt when she couldn't reconcile this act of vandalism and the straitlaced personality of her ex-best friend. However, the fact that Nola wasn't in English class this morning just implicated her further. Nola must have been too ashamed to face Marnie, right? There couldn't be another explanation.

"Atwood looks like he's about to deliver the Gettysburg Address." Dane took Marnie's clenched fist and uncurled her fingers so that he could hold her hand. They were sitting next to each other in two folding chairs behind the thick velvet burgundy curtain, which separated them from the audience. "Could he be any more ridiculous?"

Marnie turned her head slightly to the right and saw Jeremy in the middle of mock oration, puffing his chest out and standing with his shoulders perfectly squared. He seemed so tall and confident and self-assured.

*I'd kill for that posture.*

"Are you still thinking about the poster thing?"

Dane said, pulling her hand up to his lips and kissing the top of it.

Marnie felt herself slumping forward. "I can't help it, Dane. People have been laughing at me all day, and it's just going to get worse when I go out there," she said, gesturing to the stage beyond the burgundy curtain.

This time Dane kissed her cheek. "You're going to be fine. And even if you're not, everything will work out in the end, so don't worry about it."

Instead of feeling comforted by Dane's niceties and affection, Marnie was irritated. She had been humiliated this morning and was about to get pummeled again in front of the entire student body. Why was Dane being so dismissive?

"By the way, thongs are super-sexy," Dane joked, nudging Marnie with his knee. "Every single guy in your class will vote for you strictly based on that."

Marnie tried hard not to laugh, but she couldn't help it. "You're so gross."

"You like me because I'm gross." Dane put his arm around her and gave her a quick squeeze.

Suddenly, the curtains parted and Principal Baxter emerged. He was an exceptionally tall man who had recently invested in hair plugs and apparently expected nobody to notice.

"Good afternoon, students," he said into the microphone at the podium.

Marnie took a deep breath as Principal Baxter welcomed everyone and explained the next few stages of the election. Dane leaned over and kissed Marnie delicately on her cheek, which sent such a rush of excitement through her that she almost forgot to be anxious.

But that moment of serenity didn't last long. As soon as the candidates were asked to take their seats on stage, Marnie's heart rate spiked. Once they were settled in their chairs that faced the student body, Jeremy Atwood was called to the podium.

Marnie sighed heavily. She was hoping to go first so she could get it over with, but now she had to watch Jeremy set the bar for her and the rest of his opponents. And did he set the bar Sears-Tower high — Jeremy flipped through his index cards without stumbling over his words once and spoke on a wide range of issues with such authority, even Marnie was contemplating voting for him.

"As your class treasurer, I wouldn't take my responsibilities lightly," Jeremy read from his last index card with conviction. "And as voters, you shouldn't, either. Pick the best person on the ballot, not the *prettiest* or the *most popular*. Thank you."

Marnie squirmed uncomfortably in her seat as

Jeremy was hailed with a nice round of applause. But when she looked into the audience and saw Lizette smiling and waving at her, bubbles of hope rose inside Marnie's heart.

*You can do this, you're a winner,* she chanted in her mind.

"Next up, Marnie Fitzpatrick," Principal Baxter said.

Marnie got up from her seat and smoothed out her skirt with one hand while she clutched her index cards with the other. She strolled over to the podium with a big smile, mostly because she'd heard Dane whisper, "You're so gorgeous," when she'd passed by. It was just the ego boost she needed. Jeremy could preach all he wanted to about voting for the "best person" for the job, but who was he kidding? The prettiest and most popular people always seemed to come out on top in these situations.

As Marnie set her cards down on the podium and leaned toward the microphone, she hoped her fellow classmates would see things that way, too.

But then Marnie heard it.

A loud, coarse cough followed by the words, *thong thief.*

Marnie's eyes darted around the crowd, trying to find the culprit, but the only thing she saw was Sawyer Lee turning around in his seat, searching the group for the same reason, and Brynne Callaway, smiling happily as though she were enjoying the show.

Marnie shook her head and began her speech. "Fellow freshmen, I'd like to take this opportunity to —"

"Show you my thong!" someone in the bleachers blurted out.

The crowd erupted in laughter while Marnie's hands shook in fear.

"Keep going," she heard Dane whisper behind her.

Marnie heeded his advice and swallowed hard. "I'd like to take this opportunity to tell you about why I'm the best candidate for class —"

"Thong stealer!" another voice called out.

More laughter echoed through the auditorium even louder than before. Marnie tried to not to lose it, but she could feel her lower lip trembling and her legs were about to give out on her.

Suddenly, Principal Baxter came to her side. He pulled the microphone to the right so he could address the students. "If I hear one more comment from the audience, everyone, and I mean — everyone — will have restricted lunch periods and study halls for a week."

A hush fell over the crowd as Principal Baxter told Marnie she could continue.

Marnie tried to collect herself and soldier on as if

nothing had happened. She even tried fixing her eyes on a sympathetic-looking Lizette for the remainder of her speech. But the next four minutes were a disaster for Marnie. Not only did she manage to shuffle her cards so they were out of order, but she was stammering so much that she was sure people were going to stop calling her Thong Thief and start calling her Porky Pig.

The nail in the coffin, though, was when Marnie said she was against "class dudes" instead of "class dues," which ignited another wave of chuckling from her classmates. She was so out of sorts that she skipped two index cards just to get to the closing line: "Vote for Marnie Fitzpatrick, the majority leader of the Fun Party."

But when Marnie slunk back to her seat, she didn't feel like the leader of anything. She felt like a loser, and as usual, her ex-best friend was to blame.

As Marnie wiped at her eyes, she swore that the next time she saw Nola James — whether it be in school or on the street — she would meet Marnie's wrath.

# Chapter 24

On Friday morning, Nola had somehow convinced her mother that she needed to stay home another day because she was too torn up about Marnie to face school. Maybe her mom had agreed so easily because she'd been tired from pulling a double shift at the hospital, or maybe she was just sympathetic to Nola's plight. Either way, Nola was able to hide out in her room until the start of the weekend, and for that, she would be indebted to her mother until forever.

However, although Nola was safe from Marnie-related drama for the time being, she still had to face the unbearable task of making a necklace for Riley Finnegan. Matt's girlfriend was arriving in Poughkeepsie tomorrow and the necklace had to be ready before her bus pulled into the station at 1 P.M.

After she ate a bowl of Cheerios and watched a bit of *Live with Regis and Kelly* on the white countertop TV in the kitchen, a matching pajama-and-slippers clad Nola dragged herself over to the living-room window seat and started going through her supplies.

As she peered into her clear Gladware containers, Nola thought of Riley's cocoa-colored skin tone and what type of necklace might best suit her complexion.

Nola scooped out some smooth round green beads and smaller semitranslucent purple beads, and put them into tiny clear bowls so that she could get to them easily. Then she found a delicate silver chain that would lie flat against Riley's dainty collarbone.

Nola spent a good amount of time examining each bead as she strung them together, carefully eyeing every piece for flaws or imperfections that might be visible. Nola thought about the last piece of jewelry she had made: Marnie's bracelet. Nola could vividly recall every hour she put into constructing it and how excited she had been about giving it to her friend.

As Nola threaded the first bead on Riley's necklace, she wondered what Marnie thought of her now. Surely, she had assumed that Nola was behind the destruction of her posters. Did that mean Nola had gone from ex-best friend to bitter enemy? And if so, would the cold war that had lingered between her and Marnie turn into a gruesome, bitter feud that would be passed down through the generations?

Nola shook her head and tried to shift her thoughts but the only other person she could think of was Matt. Memories flooded through her head, from the first time she met him in homeroom to yesterday, when he sat beside her in Mrs. Mulchahy's office and swore that he hadn't betrayed her trust. But Nola had gone over the facts repeatedly since then and it just didn't add up. Matt was the only person who knew about Marnie's thong-inspired kleptomania. Who else could she point a finger at?

Just then, a sickening theory wedged itself in Nola's mind.

*What if Matt hadn't told anyone at all? What if he vandalized Marnie's posters himself?*

Nola fingered the beads in Riley's necklace to stop her hands from shaking. She had to be delirious to even consider this notion, right? The Matt Heatherly she adored would never harm and humiliate someone like that. Still, as Nola fixed a clasp to the necklace, she couldn't help but think that the rumors she refused to believe about Matt seemed a lot more plausible now.

But regardless of whether or not he was behind the latest Poughkeepsie Central scandal, Nola closed her eyes, leaned her head back against the wall, and imagined Matt giving a beautiful necklace like this to her.

The daydream transformed into a short catnap, which Nola awakened from twenty minutes later, the sound of her cell phone vibrating on top of the coffee table lulling Nola out of her slumber. When she picked it up, she thought she might be dreaming.

MATT H. was the name blinking on her caller ID.

Nola hesitated for a brief moment and then answered warily. "Hi," she croaked.

"Hey." Matt was definitely on the street somewhere. She could hear traffic whizzing by and all sorts of background noise. "Are you home right now?"

Nola's shoulders were so tense they were practically touching her ears. "Yeah. Why?"

Matt didn't reply. All Nola heard was a horn honk and then his phone cut out. She shrugged and set her phone back down. He was probably just checking on her because she wasn't in school today.

Nola checked the tiny digital clock on the DVD player, which was nestled behind a glass door in the large oak entertainment center. It was a little after 11 A.M. Nola figured she'd make her mom some breakfast before she went into work in a couple of hours. But before Nola could prepare a Southwestern-style egg white omelet (Dr. James's favorite), she had to clean up the mess she had made on the window seat. Nola poured the leftover beads back into their containers and grabbed a tiny blue gift box that she picked up at The Dreaming Goddess. She laid her latest masterpiece on the cotton square inside and closed it shut, her stomach lurching when she pictured Matt standing behind Riley, fastening the clasp near the nape of her neck.

Nola was about to retreat to the kitchen when she heard the doorbell. Her brow furrowed in confusion. Who would be at her house at this hour? When Nola opened the door, she stood there in complete shock — and in her blue snowflake T-shirt and drawstring pants pajama set.

Matt Heatherly stood on her porch with a harmonica in his hand and Juan the Whiz Kid by his side. They were both wearing black shades (even though it was overcast out) and Juan had a regular six-string guitar strapped across his chest. Matt tipped his sunglasses down so that they sat on the end of his nose and Nola stared at his gleaming hazel eyes.

"Surprise!" he said as a grin stretched across his face.

Nola forced herself to blink. "What are you doing here?"

"Isn't it obvious?" Matt quipped. "We're here to sing the blues."

*No. Freaking. WAY!*

"Are you ready, Juan?" He licked his lips as he brought the harmonica up to his mouth. "Let's kick it old school."

Nola tried to hold in her laughter as Juan churned out a classic blues riff and Matt's deepened his voice à la The Blues Brothers. But when she heard the lyrics to his song she could barely suck in air through her nose. She was laughing that hard.

*Went to school this morning,*
*But you weren't there.*
*I had a funny feeling*
*That you didn't care.*
*I tried to 'splain it before*
*Now I'll 'splain it again*
*I wouldn't do you no wrong*
*Cuz you're my bestest friend!*
*Yeah, I got the blues!*
*The Nola-hates-me blues.*
*Believe me, pretty mama,*
*What I'm telling you is truuuuue.*

When they were through, Nola applauded with enthusiasm. Matt and Juan lapped up the praise.

"Oh, my god, that was amazing!" Nola cheered, her trance broken. She was completely convinced that someone this awesome could never do anyone wrong.

"Well, it should be. We worked on that ditty for at least . . . ten minutes." Matt shoved the harmonica into the back pocket of his jeans and smiled.

Nola smiled back and crossed her arms over her chest to prevent the chill from penetrating her thin T-shirt. She was so happy right now she didn't even care that Matt was seeing her in her pajamas.

"So, do you hate me?" Matt asked. His eyebrows shot up as if he was worried that she'd say yes.

Nola's feet didn't feel big and clunky like usual. Instead, they felt light, like they were slowly being lifted off the ground. "I could never hate you," she said.

"Good," Matt replied with a sigh. "But what about Juan? He's been very upset throughout this ordeal."

Nola giggled and covered her eyes with her hand in embarrassment. "Juan and I are fine."

She heard Matt take a step forward and felt his hand wrap around hers, moving it away from her eyes and to her side, where he held it there gently. "Then we will leave you to your fake sickness," he said.

"Trust me, it isn't so fake," Nola said, gazing at a tiny freckle on Matt's cheek.

"Maybe you'll feel better after Friday movie night," Matt said. "You can pick the flick this time."

*This has to be more than what it seems. It just has to. Why else would he skip school to come over here and serenade me?*

Nola squeezed his hand, hoping that she was right. "Sounds good to me."

"Cool, I'll come over later." Matt let go and tapped Juan on the shoulder. *"Vámonos, amigo."*

Nola watched as Matt and Juan walked to their bikes, which were on her front lawn. All of her doubts about him had faded away and she was giddy with anticipation for his visit tonight. But before Nola could entertain any thoughts of romantic nuzzling in front of the TV, Matt came bounding back up the stairs of her porch.

"I almost forgot to ask. Do you have Riley's necklace ready?" he asked brightly.

Nola was brought back to reality with a tremendous crash. She almost lost her balance even though she was just standing still. "Um, yeah. Hold on, let me get it."

She staggered into the living room and snatched the box off of the window seat.

*Play it cool, Nol. And ignore that raging itching sensation that is SPREADING ALL OVER YOUR BODY!*

But all efforts to remain calm were pointless. Nola's only hope was to get out of this situation as fast as possible. She darted to the front door and slammed the box into Matt's hand with a blunt, "Here."

Matt opened the box and took out the necklace, his eyes widening. "Wow, Nola. This is . . . incredible! Honestly, it's way better than I ever imagined."

Nola knew that if she ever got the chance to kiss him she would think the exact same thing. "I'm glad you like it."

"Riley is going to trip out when she sees this." He put

the necklace back into the box and closed the lid. "I'll bring some cash with me tonight. How much do I owe you?"

As she looked into Matt's kind face, Nola realized that she couldn't even begin to put a price on that necklace. So she said, "Nothing."

Matt looked at her, stunned. "Are you sure?"

"Yeah, just take it." Nola shifted her gaze to her fuzzy slippers, which seemed abnormally enormous all of a sudden.

"Okay," he relented, putting the box in his jacket pocket. "But next time you need a favor, I'm your guy. Deal?"

Nola simply nodded her head.

Matt winked at her and dashed down the porch steps. Nola closed the front door and went to the window seat to watch him ride off on his bike with Juan in hot pursuit. Then she slunk into the kitchen and angrily broke a half dozen eggs into a mixing bowl, forgetting to separate the yolks from the whites, but remembering that Matt Heatherly never was, nor would be, hers.

Friday, September 28, 5:02 P.M.

**queenzee:** *hi!* ☺
**marniebird:** *hey, zee*
**queenzee:** *just wanted to c if u changed ur mind about the football game 2nite*
**marniebird:** *i dunno, not feeling v. school spirit-y 2day*
**queenzee:** *come on, marn. sawyer finally called and the big vote was this morning! we should B celebrating!*
**marniebird:** *well i don't need 2 celebrate. after all that happened, who in their right mind would vote 4 me?*
**queenzee:** *um, me, and like, everyone else who isn't retarded*
**marniebird:** *stop trying 2 cheer me up*
**queenzee:** *u know, if you stay home, u r letting the terrorists win*
**marniebird:** *wow, u will say anything, won't u?*
**queenzee:** *i don't like 2 give up ;-)*
**marniebird:** *i know, but i just don't want 2 deal with people and their stupid jokes*
**queenzee:** *listen, if anyone steps to u, sawyer and I will go all ninja on them.*
**marniebird:** *ok, fine!*
**queenzee:** *as grier would say, "cool beans!"* ☺
**marniebird:** *or as brynne would say, "blah blah bitch moan blah"*

IN **200** OUT

**queenzee:** *LOL*

**marniebird:** *so let me get ready and i'll meet u guys there*

**queenzee:** *just tell me 1 thing b4 u go*

**marniebird:** *sure*

**queenzee:** *what does "thong thief" mean? every time i ask u avoid the question*

**marniebird:** *i do not*

**queenzee:** *yes u do!*

**marniebird:** *it's so embarrassing*

**queenzee:** *i'm waiting . . .*

**marniebird:** *ugh, last year i got caught shoplifting at Victoria's Secret @ the Galleria*

**queenzee:** *OMG! really?*

**marniebird:** *really*

**queenzee:** *that is so kewl!!!!!!*

**marniebird:** *it is?*

**queenzee:** *did they throw u in the slammer?*

**marniebird:** *r u crazy?! no!!*

**queenzee:** *hahahaha, jk*

**marniebird:** *so c u at Wagner's Field?*

**queenzee:** *yep. go hawks!*

**marniebird:** *go hawks! bye!*

# Chapter 25

When the halftime buzzer rang out at Wagner Field, the Poughkeepsie Central Hawks were leading Mahopac High, 24–21. From the last row in the bleachers, Marnie applauded as the football players ran off to the locker room, raising their maroon-and-white helmets in the air as if they'd already won. She thought their celebratory attitude was a little presumptuous, given that there were still two more quarters left to play. Marnie knew what it was like to expect a smooth ride in the race to victory and then have someone (namely, your ex-best friend) shoot out your tires when you were a few feet away from the finish line.

"My nose is sooooo cold," Grier said, her teeth chattering.

Brynne huddled next to Grier, rubbing her hands together. "I think I have frostbite."

Dane unzipped his heavy Kenneth Cole coat, yanked up the fleece pullover he was wearing underneath, and revealed a waffle knit thermal shirt. "Ladies, let me introduce you to a concept called layering. See how Marnie has it down pat?"

Dane pulled her in for quick kiss on the lips and

smiled. Marnie grinned in return and glided a purple mitten-covered hand down Dane's flushed cheek. It was definitely the coldest night of the season and Marnie absolutely loved the fact that Dane could appreciate her windbreaker-over-hoodie-over-long-sleeved-T-shirt-over-tank-top combo as much as she did. The votes were really in now: She and Dane were made for each other.

However, by the sour expressions on Brynne's and Grier's faces, Marnie guessed that they weren't too impressed with her layering skills. After all, the girls were sans coats and dressed in glittery going-out tops and tight hoochie pants. Marnie was surprised they hadn't died of hypothermia yet.

"Well, I feel *just fine*," Lizette said sweetly as she cuddled in Sawyer's arms. The only article of weather-appropriate clothing Lizette had on was a pair of furry brown earmuffs. The rest of her outfit could be described as country club kitsch — an extremely short white tennis skirt, leopard-print cropped leggings, and an oversized crocheted wool cardigan. If it wasn't for Sawyer and his silver puffer jacket, which he was gallantly sharing, Lizette might have turned into an ice sculpture.

"I need hot cocoa," Grier whimpered. "Will someone go to the concession stand with me?"

"I'll go," Brynne said as her legs shook beneath her.

"Wait a sec." Dane shrugged off his jacket and handed it to Grier. "Take this. With the change in my pockets, you can get extra marshmallows."

Grier practically shrieked as she put it on. "Oh, my god. Thank you!"

Marnie immediately kissed Dane on the cheek and whispered into his ear, "You are *so* nice!"

"Can we go now? I'm freezing my ass off," Brynne barked.

Marnie could see that she wasn't kidding. The bluish tint to Brynne's lips was actually worrying her a little, so she unsnapped her windbreaker and offered it to Brynne. "Why don't you warm up for a while?"

But Brynne rolled her eyes and started galloping down the bleacher stairs. Grier just shrugged and followed in her footsteps. Marnie bit her lip.

*Wow, I'm* never *doing that again.*

Lizette shimmied over to Marnie and smiled slyly. "Can I borrow it then? I need to feed this salty popcorn craving and I don't want to catch a chill."

"Sure, Zee," Marnie said, smirking.

"You're such a Betty," Lizette chirped as she slipped into Marnie's jacket. Then she tottered down the bleachers in her spike-heeled ankle boots and shouted, "I'll bring you back a pretzel!"

Marnie laughed as she watched Lizette push through the crowd and catch up to Brynne and Grier, who linked arms with her the moment she appeared. Even from a higher altitude, Marnie had no trouble seeing how people practically genuflected when Lizette walked by. And why shouldn't they? Lizette was able to perform miracles like making Marnie forget about Nola and all the "thong thief" drama at school. Even though she wanted to climb to the top of Poughkeepsie Central's social order, Marnie also knew that she'd be fortunate if she ate Lizette's scraps for the rest of her life.

"Killer view, huh?"

Marnie turned slightly to her right and expected to lock eyes with her sorta boyfriend, but flinched when she saw Sawyer. She scanned the bleachers to see where Dane was hiding and noticed that he'd scurried away to talk with Tucker McFadden and a slew of other Majors who'd driven their Beemers to the game.

"Yeah, I know. You can see all the city lights." Marnie tried not to stare at the glint in Sawyer's dark eyes.

Sawyer pulled out a pack of cigarettes from inside his puffer coat, opened it, and offered one to Marnie.

"I'm trying to cut back," she joked.

Sawyer put one in his mouth. "Good for you." The flame from the lighter flickered, casting a glow on his face. "So who do you think is going to win?" he asked as he exhaled a tiny stream of smoke.

"It's a close game," Marnie said. "But I think the Hawks will come out on top."

Sawyer rocked back on his heels. "I meant the election."

*I can't believe how much I'm sweating right now. It's forty-five degrees out!*

"Um, well, I suppose, uh, whoever gets . . . the most . . . votes," Marnie stammered.

*Why, oh, why did I even leave the house tonight?*

"I hear that's how democracy works," Sawyer snickered as he took another drag.

Marnie elbowed him in the arm, but he kept laughing, which made her doubt he could feel anything through that coat. But then suddenly, Sawyer went pale and his face turned very serious.

"Oh, crap," he said as he stamped his cigarette out with his Vans.

"What's wrong?"

"Brian-freaking-Bennington."

Marnie stood on tiptoe and peered into the packed home stands. Sure enough, Brian Bennington was pounding up the bleacher stairs while everyone around him was pointing and laughing at the black circles around his eyes.

"You didn't," Marnie said, giggling.

"Shoe polish on the binoculars," Sawyer said, admiring his work. "I might not survive the retaliation, but god, was it worth it."

"What are you going to do?"

"Um . . . duck." Sawyer whipped off his puffer coat and threw it at Marnie, then lay down on the ground by her feet. "Put the coat on and stand over me so he doesn't see me."

Marnie was a jumble of nerves, but she followed Sawyer's instructions to the letter. She shoved her arms into his coat and leaped over him just as Brian got to the top of the stairs. Marnie remembered that the last time she tried to pull a stunt like this, the victim was an elderly gym teacher with a hearing problem. Although Brian's raccoon eyes made him look goofy and dumb, he was growling, and therefore seemed a lot more menacing.

"How's it going, Brian?" Marnie screeched. Sawyer tugged on the hem of her jeans, which she figured was code for *Shut the hell up, moron!*

"Have you seen Sawyer?" Brian snapped.

"Sawyer who?"

The tug on Marnie's jeans had turned into a hard yank.

"Sawyer Lee? You're wearing his jacket?"

*Huh, he really is smarter than Grams.*

"Oooooh, him. Well, I forgot my coat, so Saywer lent me his and then he went home to get another one," Marnie said quickly. "Can I take a message?"

Sawyer almost pulled Marnie down with that last tug.

"Yeah, let him know that the next time I see him, his ass is *mine!*" Brian said before bounding down the bleacher stairs.

Marnie immediately tapped Sawyer with the back of her foot when she saw Brian enter the men's room. "Okay, the coast is clear."

Sawyer popped up and brushed himself off. "Thanks, double-oh-seven."

Marnie punched Sawyer playfully on the arm, and since she had his coat on, she knew he could feel it. "Whatever, I totally saved your butt, jerk."

Sawyer smiled widely and then poked her in the shoulder. Marnie struck back with a knee to his hip. Sawyer got brazen and started to tickle Marnie at her sides.

"What's going on?"

Marnie's and Sawyer's heads both snapped to attention when they heard Lizette's voice coming from two bleacher steps below them.

*Oh, no. Oh, no. OOOOOOH, NOOOOOO!!!*

"Nothing," Sawyer said casually. "Marnie just got cold without her coat so I let her wear mine."

Marnie wished she could be as calm as Sawyer under these circumstances, but she was fidgeting so much, Lizette had to assume something was up. Marnie glanced over to Brynne, whose eyebrows were raised high in suspicion, and then to Grier, who was nervously twirling a strand of hair around her finger.

Lizette handed the popcorn and pretzel she was holding to Sawyer and tore off Marnie's coat in a huff. "Here ya go."

Marnie peeled off Sawyer's jacket and exchanged it with Lizette. "Thanks, Zee."

Lizette coughed up a sarcastic-sounding laugh and then turned her back to Marnie. Sawyer gave Lizette the popcorn and pretzel as he put on his coat. Then he opened it up a little so Lizette could cuddle up next to him.

"Hope you're hungry," Lizette said, offering the pretzel to Sawyer.

Marnie's body felt so hot, she wanted to rip her coat to shreds.

"So anything interesting happen while we were gone?" Brynne asked Marnie with a sneer.

But Lizette didn't give Marnie a chance to answer. "Maybe she went back to Vicky's and stole some more thongs."

Marnie crossed her arms over her chest so that no one could see the mark from the blow Lizette just dealt her.

"What?" Brynne said, snorting with laughter.

"Go ahead, tell her, Marnie." Lizette's face looked so hard right now, Marnie could barely recognize her. Or speak. "*Fine,* I will."

Marnie steeled herself. It was obvious Lizette's ego was bruised when she saw Marnie and Sawyer messing around. She would just have to sit here and take her punishment and then apologize when she and Lizette were alone. The only thing Marnie had to do was explain all that to her stomach, which was currently turning into a ball of fire.

But before Lizette could say another word, Sawyer leaned in and kissed Lizette on the mouth, thereby saving Marnie from further humiliation, even if it was only temporary. When Sawyer finally let Lizette come up for a breath, she was so dizzy and glassy-eyed that she just stood there, dumbfounded.

Thankfully, Dane rejoined their little huddle, chatted with Sawyer about passing plays, and held Marnie's hand. When it became clear to Brynne that she wasn't going to hear any more of Marnie's story, she sat down, shivering, and sulked. Grier offered Dane his coat back, but he refused and said it gave him a good reason to hug Marnie for the rest of the game, which he did.

An hour or so later, the Hawks won the game with a frantic Hail Mary pass, but Marnie couldn't celebrate with the rest of the team's elated fans. Lizette had left with Sawyer, Brynne, and Grier early in the fourth quarter because she thought she was "coming down with something," leaving Marnie to wonder just how long her friend would be mad at her.

# Chapter 26

Nola's house was twins-, parents-, and Ian-free at seven o'clock, which was around the time Matt was supposed to arrive for Friday movie night. Nola was upstairs in her room, standing in front of her full-length mirror and smoothing her hair out with the flat iron that Marnie had let her borrow on the second day of school. After she finished, Nola inspected her outfit and smirked when she imagined what Marnie would have said about it. "Pants *again?*" would probably have been the first comment out of her ex-best friend's mouth. Followed by "Nola, you can fit *both of us* in that sweater" and "Are you dressing like a boy just to drive me crazy?"

Nola heaved a big sigh. Now that there had been a fiasco at school with the posters, Nola knew that another confrontation with Marnie was imminent, regardless of who was really at fault. Nola also knew that there would be no turning back after that. She and Marnie would never, *ever* be friends again, and there wasn't anything she or anyone else could do to prevent it.

A knock at the front door pulled Nola from her thoughts.

*Oh, my god. He's here.*

Somewhere during the process of baking her second

batch of Rice Krispie Treats, Nola had convinced herself that tonight was her one chance to show Matt that he belonged with *her*. She wasn't going to come on strong, of course. That would only backfire with a shy person like Nola. No, she planned on taking a more subtle route, which involved a little bit of flirting and a serving or two of the organic Rice Krispie Treats she'd spent two hours slaving over.

But the true ace in the hole was the movie that Nola had picked out — *A Lot Like Love* starring Ashton Kutcher and Amanda Peet. Sure, it was a bit obvious (and sappy), but Nola figured, why not try to inspire Matt to look at his "bestest" friend in a romantic way on the night before his real girlfriend came to visit him? It seemed to make perfect sense!

Nola popped off the cap of her Blue Crazeberry ChapStick and ran the balm over her lips. Then Nola flew down the stairs, taking them two at a time with her eight-and-a-half-size Skechers.

When she reached the door, Nola's pulse had quickened to the point where she felt light-headed, so she took a couple of deep breaths. Unfortunately, after Nola opened the door, she realized that it would take much more than breathing techniques to combat her anxiety.

Matt looked absolutely fantastic. He'd gone through the trouble of putting some goop in his hair so that it appeared sculpted instead of messy. He was wearing a gray short-sleeve T-shirt with the CBGB emblem on it over a black long-sleeve T-shirt that was frayed at the cuffs. His dark indigo jeans that hung down around his hips were definitely brand-new.

However, the real reason Nola was utterly dumb-struck was that Riley Finnegan was standing right next to Matt, holding his hand and wearing the beaded necklace Nola had made.

"Guess who showed up early to surprise me?" Matt's face was beaming.

*Kill me now. By any means necessary.*

Riley piped up. "I hope you don't mind me crashing movie night, Nola. I just couldn't wait to get here."

Nola checked out Riley from the top of her black corkscrew curls to the bottom of her fuzzy Eskimo boots. Her skin tone was a bit darker than in her pictures, but so radiant that it actually glowed. Her brown eyes had an almost magical glint to them, her smile was warm and friendly, and although her mohair sweater and skinny jeans outfit seemed more trendy than alterna-rocker, her short fingernails were painted black, which gave her all the street cred she needed.

"I guess I should have called first," Matt said, his eyebrows arching with concern.

Nola shook herself out of her silent stupor. "That's okay. Come on in."

As she showed them to the living room, Nola shoved her hands back in her pockets so no one could see them trembling. Matt and Riley dodged all of Dennis and Dylan's toys and sat down on the couch.

"It's nice to finally meet you, Nola," Riley chirped. "Matt's told me so much, I feel like we're friends already."

Nola forced a smile. *Oh, my god! What a phony! How could Matt even* like *this girl?*

"So where are Dennis and Dylan?" Matt asked as he put his arm around Riley. "Holding the manny hostage?"

Nola was sure her knuckles were turning white. "Ian took them to the comic book store."

Riley grinned at Matt and ruffled his hair. "Aw, that sucks, babe. I was hoping they'd be around to kick your ass so I could watch and cheer them on."

Matt laughed and nuzzled Riley's neck. "Well, maybe you and I could wrestle instead. Whaddya say, Nola? Wanna ref?"

Now Nola's blood was boiling. How could Matt be so insensitive? Was he *blind*? Didn't he see how hard it was for Nola to even *hear* about Riley, let alone *meet* her and watch him *nuzzle her neck*? Nola was in an elevated zone of angry that she'd never experienced before, which is why she had to do something — right now — or else she might leap onto the couch and beat the two of them to a pulp.

"I made Rice Krispie Treats!" Nola exclaimed as if she'd discovered a new fuel source that would end the U.S. dependency on oil.

Riley covered her mouth and giggled. "Oh, my god, Matt, remember Rooney Fest, when we made —"

"S'mores?" Matt finished Riley's sentence while chuckling and shifting his arm so his hand was on her waist. "I still have nightmares about that campfire."

"Next time we're in the sleeping bag, we'll have to make sure the kerosene isn't so close to our feet," Riley said as she touched the tip of Matt's nose.

Nola swallowed hard. "I'm going to the kitchen. Be right back!"

Matt started to get up. "Need any help, Nol?"

"No, I've got it, thanks," she said and faked another smile before sprinting into the kitchen.

In the split-second it took Nola to get from one room to the other, she considered opening the oven, turning on the gas, and sticking her head in. How was she going to get through the night like this? Or more importantly, how was she going to be able to get through *freshman year* like this — being Matt's friend when she wanted way more than that?

But every thought was wiped from Nola's mind when

she got to the kitchen and saw Ian, Dennis, and Dylan gorging themselves on her Rice Krispie Treats. Dennis was licking his fingers and Dylan was wiping his hands on his dirty pants as Ian popped a bite in his mouth.

Nola gritted her teeth. "What. Are. You. Fools. Doing?"

"Having a snack?" Ian said, chewing.

"How did you even get in here?"

"The back door," he explained. "I didn't want these guys tracking dirt through the house. Are you okay?"

Nola was breathing so hard she thought she might faint. "No, I'm not! I have people over and those treats were for *them*!"

Ian's face drooped. "Oh. Sorry."

Nola scowled and tapped her foot as if she was waiting for a more heartfelt apology, but it didn't come. Not by a long shot.

"What are you so bent out of shape about? The boys are *quiet* for once. Doesn't that make you *happy*?" Ian got up and went to the refrigerator to fetch a carton of skim milk.

"Yeah, but they'll be bouncing off the walls when that sugar high kicks in," Nola snapped. "And I have guests who'd rather not be assaulted with Creepy Crawlers!"

"Then take them up to your room!" Ian snapped back.

"*Fine!* I will!" Nola said as she stormed over to the pantry and grabbed a huge bag of Baked! Lay's Potato

Crisps. At the moment, she didn't think there was anything or anyone she could hate more than Ian Capshaw, the most inconsiderate, obnoxious boy she'd ever laid eyes on.

Until she stood in the doorframe of the living room a moment later, and laid her eyes on Riley and Matt, who were kissing on the sofa.

Nola was so enraged that she squeezed the potato chip bag really hard, which made a loud crunching sound that startled Riley and Matt. They broke away from each other and sprang to opposite sides of the couch like they'd been caught in the act by one of their parents.

"Yikes, Nol, I had no idea you were there," Matt said, wiping his mouth with the back of his hand.

*Yeah, tell me about it,* Nola thought.

Riley giggled uncomfortably. "You know how guys are. They only have one thing on their mind."

"What? *You* pounced on *me!*" Matt proclaimed.

Regardless of how much she wanted to hurl right now, Nola knew one thing for sure: She despised Riley Finnegan. *Intensely.*

"Oooooh, Baked! Lay's," Riley said, changing the subject. "Are those sour cream and onion?"

Nola looked down and prayed they were barbecue-flavored. But no go. "Yes, they are," she said with a sigh.

"Sweet!" Riley shouted as she leaped up from the

couch and dashed over to Nola. She cupped her hands together and waited for Nola to pour some chips into her palms, but Nola just shoved the bag at her and retreated to the window seat in frustration.

"So, what's the movie tonight, Miss James?" Matt asked.

Riley plopped down next to Matt again and offered the bag to him. "Hopefully something with gallons of blood and guts."

"Oh, I'm definitely in the mood for gore," Matt said before popping a chip in his mouth.

Nola bowed her head in shame. How could she possibly watch *A Lot Like Love,* or anything else for that matter, with her romantic rival sitting on the other side of her soul mate?

"Um, our DVD players are having . . . technical difficulties," she mumbled.

Riley smirked. "Should we, like, stand by?"

"Ha! That was awesome," Matt laughed.

*Huh? She's not even funny!*

"Actually, I think we should call off the movie," Nola said, her eyes cascading down to Riley's small, dainty feet. It then occurred to her that she had no choice but to keep lying her way out of this impossible situation. "I forgot that my dad is coming back from a long business trip tonight, and it's probably not a good time to have people over."

Matt's face fell in disappointment. "Oh, okay."

"I'm sorry," Nola murmured.

"No worries. Maybe we could hang out tomorrow night," Riley said with a smile.

*This. Girl. SUCKS!*

"You know what? Evan Sanders's brother told him there's supposed to be a dope party tomorrow night," Matt said with a spark of enthusiasm. "Why don't we all go?"

Nola furrowed her brow. Was Matt suggesting they crash somebody's party? Wasn't that against the rules or something?

"Yes! I'm totally down for a soiree," Riley chimed in.

The pressure in the air was tangible, but Nola was not about to attend a party she wasn't invited to, let alone attend with the boy she liked and the girl she loathed.

The perfect "no" was formulating in Nola's brain when Matt got up, crossed the room, knelt down in front of her, and said, "Please say you'll come, Nola."

In seconds, the perfect *no* transformed into a messy *yes*, a decision that Nola knew would bite her in the rear end.

It was only a matter of time.

# Chapter 27

Zee's Recent Mood Swings: A Detailed List Compiled on
Saturday, September 29

1.  After she left the football game and ignored all my
    text messages, Zee called me today and asked if I was
    going to this party at Deirdre's house tonight. Zee
    sounded really happy, as if nothing was wrong, until I
    mentioned that Deirdre hadn't invited me, and then
    she said, "Oh, that's right. Deirdre said it was for
    CLOSE friends only. You probably shouldn't come
    then."

2.  Zee kept asking me to tell her more about the Thong
    Thief story, which I really didn't want to do, consid-
    ering that she used it against me last night when
    she was pissed off about Sawyer (ugh, I wish my
    stomach would stop fluttering when I think about
    him). However, I figured it couldn't hurt to humor
    her, so I mentioned that Nola was at the scene of the
    crime and was the only one who knew about it, which
    meant Nola had to be the person who destroyed my
    posters. All of a sudden, Zee was up in arms over the
    whole thing, most likely because she worked hard on
    those posters and was angry as hell that someone

had ruined them (she never liked Nola to begin with, and honestly, I don't blame her). But then Zee calmed down and said she had my back if Nola pulled any more stunts. I was stunned — just a few minutes before, Zee was giving me a hard time about Deirdre's party and now she was so interested in protecting me.

3. By the end of the conversation, Zee was begging me to come to Deirdre's party with Dane and apologizing for being bitchy to me last night. I accepted, of course.

"Just a little while longer," Dane said as he leaned Marnie against the slew of expensive coats in Deirdre Boyd's hallway closet. He was kissing her ear and working his way over to her lips with tiny pecks that tickled Marnie's skin like a feather. She had to admit, even though she didn't want to play this ridiculous old-fashioned game, seven minutes in the closet wasn't even close to enough time when it came to kissing Dane Harris.

Marnie gently tugged on his lower lip with her teeth and cupped his face in her hands. "There are people waiting to get in here, you know. We shouldn't be greedy."

"Let them wait. I like having you all to myself." Dane clutched at Marnie's hips.

"I like it, too," she murmured, trailing her fingers down his back.

Suddenly, the door flew open and Marnie and Dane were blinded by bright track lighting.

"Oh, *god*, could you two take your groping elsewhere?"

It was Brynne Callaway, and she didn't look happy. In fact, the best way to describe the expression on Brynne's face was profoundly disgusted and deeply annoyed, but that wasn't out of the ordinary.

Dane straightened up and walked out of the closet, holding Marnie by the hand. Brynne budged by the both of them and grabbed a cropped tweed blazer off one of the hangers, stuffing her arms into the sleeves.

"Leaving so soon?" Marnie asked as she adjusted her grape-colored off-the-shoulder mohair sweater, which Dane had somehow managed to twist up.

"Yeah, this party reeks." A bead of spittle flew out from the gap in between Brynne's front teeth.

"Really?" The corners of Marnie's mouth twitched into a smile as she gazed at Dane. "I'm having fun."

Brynne rolled her eyes. "Well, you know me. Blah blah bitch moan blah," she scoffed.

Marnie's head snapped back as if she'd been slapped. Lizette had gone and told Brynne what Marnie had said during their IM conversation the other day! Wasn't that supposed to be a private joke? How could Lizette be so careless, especially when she knew that Marnie and Brynne didn't get along?

Marnie tried to appease Brynne, whose face was bright red and pinched. "I was only kidding when I said that, Brynne."

Brynne buttoned up her jacket and swung her extra-large studded white hobo bag over her shoulder. "Your friend Nola was right. You are such a *wannabe*, it seriously makes me want to puke."

With that insightful comment, Brynne stomped out of Deirdre's faux château home on Eastman Terrace and slammed the door behind her.

Dane scratched his head in confusion. "What was that about?"

"Brynne just wants my head on a platter, that's all." Marnie tried to make sure her voice sounded upbeat, but she knew that Dane wouldn't buy it.

"Don't worry about her," Dane said, pulling Marnie in for a warm hug. "She's probably just jealous of you."

*Maybe*, Marnie thought. But that didn't explain why Lizette had gone off and told Brynne that Marnie had been making fun of her.

"Listen, why don't I get us some drinks?" Dane led Marnie through a crowd of people in the foyer to

Deirdre's kitchen, nodding his head in time to the pumping bass of a Jay-Z song.

Marnie sighed. How come Dane was so fixated on drinking every time they went to a party? "Actually, I think I'm going to find Zee and see what she's up to."

"Okay. I'll hook up with you later," Dane said as he high-fived a few of his guy friends from student council and grabbed a can of beer.

Marnie gave Dane a half-grin and edged her way through all of Poughkeepsie Central's prettiest rich girls and hottest rich boys. She stopped when she reached the center of the humongous, elegant living area, which had a baby grand piano in one corner and a looming, ornate grandfather clock in the other. As Marnie glanced around the packed room, she thought about Brynne calling her a wannabe and it made a surge of insecurity rip through her.

After all the ups and downs of the past few weeks, Marnie thought that she'd feel a lot more sturdy and confident, especially when it came to Lizette. And she had, until that stupid football game. Marnie wanted to kick herself while wearing steel-toed work boots for acting all silly with Sawyer. Sure, she hadn't meant anything by it, but for some reason, Lizette had seemed to think Marnie was enjoying Sawyer's attention a little too much.

But what really shook Marnie up was the realization that there might be some truth to that.

"Are you having a good time?" Lizette appeared next to Marnie.

Marnie smirked when she got a good look at Lizette's getup: zebra print formal shorts over fuchsia tights paired with a powder blue ruffled tuxedo shirt. "Yeah, I guess."

"Um, hel-*lo*? You just got freaky with Dane in a closet. You should be psyched!" Lizette enthused.

"Well, I had a baby catfight with Brynne," Marnie said, gauging whether or not Lizette would cop to selling Marnie out on her own.

Instead of admitting that she snitched, Lizette started engaging in one of her worst habits — shoulder surfing. "Brynne's just in one of her moods. You know how she is."

"Right." Marnie's heart sank a little.

A sinister smile suddenly formed on Lizette's face, as if she was about to spread an unbelievable rumor. "I'm so bummed that Sawyer isn't here. He's going to miss all the fun."

Marnie's wrinkled her nose. "What do you mean?"

Lizette jutted her chin out in the direction of the foyer, where a familiar looking guy was hanging up some coats in the infamous makeout closet. Marnie's breath caught in her throat when she realized that guy was Matt Heatherly. A pretty black girl with curly hair took his arm, and then Marnie's worst night terror came true. Her ex-best friend Nola James came into view.

"What is *she* doing here?" Marnie felt a hot flash zap her body with such intensity that she almost dropped to her knees.

"That doesn't matter, does it?" Lizette asked slyly. "All I know is you should smack her for what she did to you."

Marnie clenched her fists as she watched an unsuspecting Nola slink away with the mystery girl as Matt led them off toward the kitchen. "I think you're right."

"Good," Lizette said, putting her arm around Marnie and giving her a big squeeze. "You just need to wait for the right moment."

But there was just one problem. Marnie was sick to death of being patient where Nola was concerned, so whether the moment was right or wrong, Marnie was going to strike at the first opportunity.

After all, there was no etiquette when it came to revenge.

# Chapter 28

As Nola stood next to Riley in the smoky, yet pristinely decorated den of some stranger's house, she asked herself repeatedly what kind of greater force was at work when she had told Matt that she'd attend this "crunked-out" party with him and his girlfriend. Had it been the dark magic of the full moon that made Nola cave into Matt's pleading? Or was she easily swayed due to a mental break-down caused by watching Matt and Riley lip-locked?

Either way, Nola had agreed to this little outing, regardless of how idiotic the idea seemed, and she couldn't bail out now, even though she'd nearly hyper-ventilated when she saw how many kids were milling about, sipping on drinks in plastic cups, and moving their hips to the earsplitting music.

Nola could see it in the partygoers' caustic stares that she didn't belong there. But when she glanced at Riley, who was wearing a pirate-inspired bandanna, form-fitting baby T-shirt, and weather-beaten Citizen jeans, Nola knew without a doubt that if her current sidekick went to Poughkeepsie Central, she'd be an integral member of this in-crowd.

As Nola watched Riley shimmy about, she wished she was shoving straight pins into a voodoo doll.

"This playlist is so fetch," Riley said as she swung her hips back and forth. "Don't you just love how we went from Jay-Z to The Pixies? What a segue! I wonder who the DJ is."

"Me, too," Nola said in agreement, even though she was trying hard to tune Riley out.

Riley's dark eyes moved from left to right, scanning the crowd with excitement. "Sorry, we never have parties like this in Westwood. You must go to these things all the time, right?"

Given Nola's stiff, closed-off posture, she wondered how Riley could have even asked that question. Was this chick the least observant person in the tristate area? When Nola looked down at her gray drawstring velveteen cargo pants and her beige-and-white striped shawl sweater, she was surprised Riley hadn't asked her if it was laundry day. "Um, actually, I don't go out that much."

*Great, now I sound like an agoraphobic loser.*

Riley nudged Nola good-naturedly. "Well, I'm glad you made an exception for tonight. I *love* being with Matt and all, but it's nice to spend time with a girl."

Nola sighed. Whenever she was around Matt, the last thing she wanted to do was share him with anyone else, least of all someone like Riley. Didn't this girl know how insanely good she had it?

"Hey, Nola, I know we just met and everything,"

Riley said, gliding her slender fingers over her necklace. "But before Matt comes back with our drinks, I wanted to thank you for being his friend. He and I are away from each other a lot and I can't always be there for him. But knowing you're around when I'm not makes me so, I don't know, relieved, I guess."

Nola's eyebrows raised in bewilderment. She could take Riley's comment as a gracious token of appreciation, or she could interpret it as a total slam. Riley was *relieved* that Nola was around Matt when she couldn't be with him? Come on! That had to mean Riley thought Nola was some kind of dog-faced loser that Matt would never be attracted to in a zillion years. Didn't it?

While Nola stood there, trying to make sense of Riley's intentions, Riley went on. "I'm sure you know that he's been through some hard times with the police investigation starting up again and everything, so he can use all the friends he can get."

*What?! He's in trouble with the* police?

Nola wanted to grab Riley by her twiggy arms and shake her until she spilled the beans. But Nola's plot was sabotaged when Riley said she needed to fix one of her contacts and went in search of a bathroom. Considering how gigantic Deirdre's house was, Riley could be gone for hours, if not days.

Surprisingly, Nola was so preoccupied with what Riley had said about Matt, that she wasn't even worried that she'd been stranded in the den with a bunch of strangers who were glaring at her. All she could think about was what could have happened to Matt that drove him to do something that got him kicked out of school and garnered the attention of the police. Nola was in a daze, contemplating possible circumstances, but what bothered her more than anything was that Matt hadn't told her himself about his misdeeds. It seemed as though both Iris and Riley were positive that Nola already knew. So why didn't she? Why was Matt keeping secrets from her?

All of these thoughts were really weighing on Nola, which is why someone had to shove her hard to make her snap out of her dream state. When Nola tumbled back to reality, she was peering into the angry eyes of her ex-best friend.

"If you think you can humiliate me at school and then show up here at this party uninvited," Marnie shouted above the music, "you must *really* have a death wish."

Nola was so shocked that all she could get out was a meek spurt of noise that sounded like, *"Wha?"*

"Oh, so you're going to play it like you didn't write that junk all over my posters? I *know* it was you!" Marnie yelled again as the music volume lowered and everyone in the den gathered around.

Although Nola was sure this moment would come, she hadn't prepared for it in the least. She was certain that if she admitted to telling Matt the Thong Thief story, but denied ruining Marnie's posters, the suspicion would immediately shift toward Matt. Besides, given what Riley had said a few minutes ago, there was even more reason to believe that Matt had been involved. Still, even with more than fifty pairs of eyes watching her every move, Nola had to dig deep and gather her courage, reminding herself that no matter what happened, she had someone to lean on for support, even though that someone had a hot girlfriend and was totally MIA at the moment.

"You don't know *squat*, Marnie," Nola snapped. "And if you think I'd waste my time messing with your *lame* posters, you must be as dumb as you look!"

Everyone in the crowd let out a collective "Ooooooh."

Marnie narrowed her eyes and sneered. "*I* look dumb? Please, you should see the way you trail Matt Heatherly around like a stupid lovesick puppy. I would feel sorry for you if you weren't such a *backstabber!*"

Nola felt as though Marnie had hit her in the stomach with a sledgehammer. Marnie had just told everyone in the room about her crush on Matt! What if he had been in earshot? Or what if Riley heard and was on her way to tell him? How could Nola ever face Matt again? Still, as terrified as she was of the truth being out there, Nola pushed herself to take Marnie on.

"Well, maybe *I* would feel sorry for *you* if you weren't such a *coldhearted wench*!" Nola screamed as her neck became blotchy and discolored.

Marnie was about to strike back when Lizette and Matt came on the scene. They both stood by their contenders as if they were working the corners of a boxing match.

"What's going on here?" Matt asked as he tried to hold on to three plastic cups with two hands.

"Isn't it obvious?" Lizette said rather snottily. "Nola flipped out on Marnie like she *always does*."

Matt had the audacity to laugh right in Lizette's face. "Kind of like you're always so full of it?"

Nola's heart did a triple backflip. Matt was sticking up for her!

"What*ever*," Lizette said, scowling. "Can you and your skanks see yourselves out, or do I need to draw you a map?"

Another "ooooh" echoed throughout the room, this one louder than before. But that didn't faze Matt. He stood there confidently as Riley emerged from the crowd and quietly ambled up beside him.

"Nah, we'll be fine, Lizette. Thanks for your concern," he said, shoving three cups of soda into Marnie's unwitting hands so hard that some of the contents spilled onto her outfit and the Indian rug underneath her feet.

Then Matt took Nola by the hand and led her out of the house while Riley followed behind, their coats weighing her down so she couldn't keep up with them.

**mheatherly:** *hey, nol. how r u?*

**nolaj1994:** *ok, i suppose*

**mheatherly:** *sorry about the party last nite, i had no idea that marnie was going 2 b there*

**nolaj1994:** *it wasn't ur fault*

**mheatherly:** *still, i feel bad u had to go thru all that*

**nolaj1994:** *well i feel bad that u and riley had to leave. she seemed 2 b having a good time*

**mheatherly:** *no worries, she and i understood*

**nolaj1994:** *thx. how was the rest of ur weekend 2gether?*

**mheatherly:** *great, actually. after riley and i dropped u off at ur place, we went 2 Overlook 4 some mini golf, and this morning we had 2 rooty tooty fresh 'n fruity breakfasts @ IHOP. now she's on the bus headed back 2 westwood*

**nolaj1994:** *sounds nice*

**mheatherly:** *yeah, it was. i can't believe how much i miss her after only a couple hrs*

**nolaj1994:** *well u 2 will visit again soon, right?*

**mheatherly:** *true, but who knows what could happen between now and then? 1 minute someone is in ur life, and the next minute the same person can drift out of it and never come back*

**nolaj1994:** *well u know riley better than i do, but she doesn't strike me as the type of girl who would just disappear on u*

**mheatherly:** *maybe, but it's hard not to be paranoid after everything that's happened*

**nolaj1994:** *what do u mean?*

**nolaj1994:** *matt? u still there?*

**mheatherly signed out at 1:50 P.M.**

# Chapter 29

On Monday morning, Marnie wrung her hands and paced as she waited to hear Principal Baxter announce the winners of Friday's election. When the bell for homeroom had rung a few minutes ago, she and all the other nominees had been corralled into lecture hall 4 so they could listen to the results without having to worry about censoring their reactions like celebrities do at the Oscars. Marnie wasn't worried about that too much — she had spent most of Sunday preparing for disappointment and even wrote a concession speech, although Dane had told her she wouldn't need it.

However, she was mostly anxious about letting Lizette down. On the ride to school, Lizette wouldn't stop talking about how they would celebrate Marnie's victory. Each time she mentioned a possible party location, Marnie's jaw would tighten up just thinking about how many people had laughed at her when they saw Marnie's trashed posters and how she'd humiliated herself during her speech at the assembly.

Marnie couldn't even fathom which people would pick her over Jeremy Atwood, who was poised and levelheaded throughout his campaign, or even the other two candidates, Michelle Weaver and Julianna Pescatore, who'd handed out homemade cookies and glitter pens, respectively. Every student in the freshman class would have had to come down with some contagious form of amnesia for any of them to check off the box by Marnie Fitzpatrick's name.

"Don't you wish we were back in Deirdre's closet?" Dane said as he came up from behind and wrapped his arms around her.

Marnie wanted to wiggle away from him, but instead she just stayed still and tried to put thoughts about Saturday night out of her mind. She was still pretty pissed that Nola had the gall to show up at that party after what she'd done to Marnie's posters. If it hadn't been for Nola, Marnie wouldn't even have to worry about losing this election. However, when Marnie felt Dane's lips graze the back of her earlobe, she couldn't help but feel a little warmer all over.

Dane spun her around with his hands and smiled at her wickedly. He was wearing a gray ribbed turtleneck sweater with the sleeves pushed up and Marnie noticed that he'd just gotten a haircut, which made him even more gorgeous than the first — and only — time she'd seen him (by accident) in his underwear. "You didn't answer me," he said, stepping back and putting his hands on his hips.

"Sorry," Marnie replied as she yanked up one of her patterned knee socks and straightened her pleated mini. "I'm just —"

"Vexed?"

Marnie gave him a curious look.

"PSAT word." Dane's grin always packed such a punch.

Everyone snapped to attention when Principal Baxter's voice sounded over the loud speaker.

*"Good morning, students. The results of Friday's election have been tabulated."*

Dane immediately took Marnie's hand, brought it up to his mouth, and kissed the tips of her fingers. Then he mouthed the words, "Don't worry." Marnie was amazed — all Dane had to do was one sweet thing and she was reduced to Silly Putty.

*"I will reveal the winners by class, starting with freshmen."*

Marnie's eyes darted over to Jeremy Atwood, who was sitting down in the front row of the lecture hall with his head bowed and his hands clasped.

*Wait, is he praying?*

When she craned her neck a little bit, she saw Jeremy's thin lips moving slightly. This was so odd. It didn't take a pollster to figure out that Jeremy had become the front-runner after their speeches on Thursday. Why was he even sweating this thing?

*"Secretary, Kim Tremont."*

A bubbly auburn-haired girl who was crouched down behind the podium jumped up and squealed. It startled Jeremy so much that he jerked in his chair. Now that he was looking up, Marnie could see that he really *was* sweating. Marnie was nervous about losing, but when she saw how much Jeremy was agonizing over this, she wondered if she was the right person for the job.

*"Treasurer, Marnie Fitzpatrick."*

Before the words had even sunk in, Dane picked Marnie up and twirled her in circles as a few people in the room clapped their hands in congratulations.

"Put me down, Dane. You're making me dizzy!" she said, giggling.

"I knew you'd win!" Dane yelped as he set Marnie on her platform boot clad feet.

At first, Marnie was in a state of disbelief — despite all the taunts during her speech, she had ended up victorious. Then the excitement began to sink in. Marnie grabbed Dane's hands and jumped up and down as if there were springs attached to her feet. But the second Marnie's gaze shot over to Jeremy, a hint of sadness took hold of her.

Jeremy was leaning back in his seat with his legs stretched out and his arms partially shielding his face. Even though Marnie was psyched about winning, she felt so bad for Jeremy that she wandered away from Dane and approached her former opponent with an out-stretched hand.

"You ran a great race, Jeremy," Marnie said sincerely.

Jeremy shoved his hands in his pockets and stared at her. "It's not fair," he muttered before getting up and brushing past Marnie.

As she watched Jeremy dash out of the room, Marnie felt a shot of anger race up her spine — how could Jeremy be so rude to her when she was just trying to be a good sport? And why was he whining about things not being fair? Marnie had been laughed at and humiliated in front of the school, and *she* wasn't complaining about how unfair that was!

But the anger Marnie was feeling somehow swelled into pride ten minutes later as she walked the halls of Poughkeepsie Central with the new sophomore vice president on her arm and people shouting congratulations as they glided by. She truly didn't think she could feel any better — that is, until she caught Nola sneering at her from behind her locker door.

When Marnie sashayed past Nola, she locked eyes with her ex-best friend and stared her down until Nola lost her edge and averted her gaze.

It was the first time Marnie ever felt invincible, and she was absolutely positive that it wouldn't be the last.

At seventh-period lunch, the only topic of discussion at anyone's table was the elections, and there was no exception at Lizette Levin's little nook in the back corner of the cafeteria. Marnie was sitting in between Lizette and Grier, enjoying every ounce of attention and praise they showered her with.

In fact, all day everyone in the freshman class had been going out of their way to tell Marnie how thrilled they were that she'd won the treasurer spot. Dane had been sending her sweet texts like U R THE BEST! and CAN'T WAIT 2 CELEBRATE all morning long, too. Marnie was so elated that she practically shrieked when Lizette said she was in the early stages of planning a huge bash in Marnie's honor.

"Omigod, Zee, you are amazing!" she yelped.

"Tell me about it," Lizette said with a sly grin and an over-the-top hair flip that made Grier giggle. "This party is going to be super-exclusive. Secret password and location. Majors only. You're going to *loooove* it."

Marnie pushed her chicken Caesar wrap to the side and smiled widely. She was so ecstatic that she couldn't even finish her food. "That sounds totally *hawt*."

"Well, you deserve it. We're so proud of you," Grier chirped before taking a sip of Diet Sprite.

"God, are you guys still talking about that dumb election?" Brynne had just come back from the bathroom and thrown her D&G bag down on her seat with contempt.

Lizette retied the silver-and-gold woven belt she'd wrapped around her canary yellow polka-dot dress and rolled her eyes at Brynne. "Actually, we're talking about Marnie's inauguration party."

Brynne put her hands on her hips and let out a sarcastic laugh. "How ridiculous."

Marnie scowled at Brynne. *This gap-toothed grinch isn't going to burst my bubble.* "Well, if you think it's ridiculous, maybe you shouldn't come," she barked.

But Brynne just ignored Marnie, unzipped her bag, and pulled out a blue heart-shaped coin purse. "I'm going to get some Little Debbie snack cakes," Brynne announced before marching off toward the vending machines.

"I think we need to take Brynne to the emergency room," Marnie said.

"Why?" Grier ask.

Marnie grinned. "So a doctor can remove whatever is stuck in her butt."

Lizette laughed so hard, she nearly spit out a mouthful of roasted almonds. "You are *so* bad!"

Grier's snickering turned her face bright red. "I can't believe you said that!"

Marnie was surprised she'd said it, too, but she didn't feel sorry about it one bit. In fact, she was glad that Lizette and Grier seemed to be on Marnie's side when Brynne was being nasty to her.

Suddenly, the Dixie Chicks' song "Not Ready to Make Nice" started blasting from Brynne's bag. Grier went through it hurriedly in search of Brynne's cell phone, the contents piling up on the table: a round hairbrush with Brynne's long auburn hair stuck in the bristles, a black Chanel compact, a silver iPod nano, and a thick purple marker that Marnie could not take her eyes off of.

"Got it!" Grier cried when she managed to locate Brynne's pocket-size Samsung. She hit the SILENCE button and then swept the rest of the contents back into Brynne's D&G bag.

When Brynne returned to the table, Marnie was in a trance. The subject had changed from the election to the latest celebrity gossip, but the discussion wasn't registering in Marnie's brain. The only thing she could think about was that purple marker and the purple words that were scrawled over her posters.

Maybe, just maybe, Nola wasn't to blame after all.

# Chapter 30

After school, Nola went straight home and changed into a pair of ratty blue sweatpants from her dad's University of Michigan days and an old, yet comfortable green T-shirt with a sizable cranberry juice stain. Then she flopped down on her bed and watched two hours' worth of TV.

By the fourth rerun of *Sabrina, the Teenage Witch*, Nola turned down the volume and buried her head in her pillow. She breathed in the scent of lavender linen mist that she sprayed on her sheets every night. Usually, this smell would lull Nola into a deep, restful sleep, but she was too worked up to even consider a nap. All she could think about was Matt.

Nola had tried calling and texting him after he suddenly logged off IM last night, but he hadn't replied. Matt hadn't been in school today, either, so of course, Nola was on the verge of losing her sanity. What could be so bad that Matt would end their conversation abruptly? Was he mad at her because she pressed him a little bit about his past? None of this made any sense, and Nola got so worked up about it that she threw her pillow across the room in frustration.

This could only mean two things: 1) Nola really was

in love, and 2) she had to stop being friends with Matt Heatherly before any permanent damage was done to her heart.

The door to her bedroom creaked open and Nola sat up to see who dared to disturb her.

*Blech. Ian.*

"Can I come in?" he asked.

Nola wanted to listen to the same inner voice that warned her about becoming best friends with Matt, but she was able to see a hint of sincere concern in Ian's green eyes, so she gave him the benefit of the doubt. "Sure."

Ian inched into the room slowly and made himself comfortable on Nola's desk chair. He rubbed his hands a few times on his Diesel jeans–clad thighs and then leaned forward so his elbows were resting on his knees. "So . . ."

"So . . ." Nola repeated.

"What are you up to?"

"Nothing."

Ian scratched the back of his neck. "Cool."

*This is a fascinating discussion.*

"Um, did you want something?" Nola asked.

"Yeah, actually," Ian said. "I wanted to tell you that I was sorry."

Nola's eyebrows shot up in surprise. "For what exactly?"

"Friday night. I was way out of line," Ian's said as his left leg bounced up and down. "When I took this job, I thought, how hard could watching two little kids be? But now it's pretty evident that I'm terrible at it."

Nola felt a smirk developing on her lips. If Ian only knew how many professional nannies their family had gone through, he probably wouldn't be so hard on himself. "Well, if it means anything, you're not worse than me."

Ian's shoulders shook a little bit as he laughed. "You sure know how to stroke a guy's ego."

Nola chuckled as she took off her wide red fabric headband and ran her fingers through her hair quickly so it fell softly around her face.

"So did you have a good weekend?" Ian asked.

Immediately, Nola's mind flashed back to her humongous blowout with Marnie on Saturday night. She was still incredibly angry at Marnie for ambushing her and acting like a psychopath just because Nola had dared to be at the same party as Marnie. Who the hell was Marnie to tell Nola where she could go and where she couldn't? Did Marnie and her stupid new friends own every square inch of Poughkeepsie now? It was enough to make Nola hive-ridden.

"It was okay," she replied. Although Ian was being civil to her at the moment, Nola didn't feel comfortable talking to him about her war with Marnie.

Ian got up from the desk chair and ambled over to Nola's window. Nola accidentally caught a glimpse of Ian's butt when he leaned forward and craned his head so he could get a better view of outside.

*Whoa*, Nola thought as she gulped hard.

"Hey, who's moving in next door?" he inquired.

"I didn't know anyone even bought that house. It's been vacant forever." Nola hopped up from her bed and stood next to Ian, who quickly moved over to the left and gave her more room.

She peered out the window at the super-size U-Haul truck that was parked on Winding Way and then shifted her gaze to the front lawn of the colonial house next door. The realtor had placed a SOLD sign on the lawn, and there were large cardboard boxes everywhere. Nola hadn't noticed that movers were milling about when she'd come home from school, so they must have shown up when she was watching TV.

"They sure have a lot of stuff," Ian said. "Maybe that family will have kids who could play with Dennis and Dylan."

Nola laughed as she pressed her hands against the glass. "Dream on, Ian."

He sighed. "You're right. Who am I kidding?"

Nola was about to pull herself away from the window when she thought she saw a familiar face. She squinted and tried to identify a tall, lanky boy with brown hair who was helping the movers out. But it wasn't his physical features that gave him away.

It was the last name printed on the back of the baseball jersey he was wearing.

Briggs.

As in Marnie Fitzpatrick's ex-boyfriend/soul mate Weston Briggs.

*H. O. L. Y. C. R. A. P.*

Before Nola could truly absorb what was happening, a loud thumping sound shook the house from the ground up.

Nola's brow crinkled. "What was that?"

"EEEEEEE-AAAAAAN!" a voice called out from the downstairs.

Ian rolled his eyes. "I better go find out." And with that, he sprinted out the door.

Nola returned her gaze to the bedroom window. She peered down at the U-Haul truck and saw Weston carrying a floor lamp. He hadn't changed one bit since he had moved away months ago. Same pretty-boy face.

Same toned muscles. Same overconfident strut. Same devilish smile.

*Oh, my god. If Marnie knew he was back in Poughkeepsie, she'd freak!*

But as Nola closed the blinds, she remembered how Marnie flaunted her election win today, strolling the halls with her jerky boyfriend as if she were better than everyone else. Then Nola recalled the harsh words and accusations Marnie had spat at her on Saturday and how Lizette Levin threw her, Matt, and Riley out of Deirdre's house, like they were rejects or something!

A blazing flash of anger lit up inside of Nola and burned right through to the skin. As she watched Weston saunter back to the truck, Nola made a solemn vow — she wasn't going to retreat from Marnie Fitzpatrick any longer. In fact, Nola promised herself that she would launch an offensive that would knock her ex-best-friend-turned-nemesis off her self-obsessed pedestal. And unlike Marnie and *her* promises, Nola planned to keep hers.

All Nola needed to do was develop a winning strategy, and thanks to Weston Briggs, she already had her first maneuver in place.

And tomorrow night, Nola was going to execute it.

# Acknowledgments

Special thanks to my editor, friend, and lamb-cheeked goddess Aimee Friedman; Scholastic's high priestess of cool Abby McAden; former-ARAP member and loyal reader Priscilla Ma; the FV Dinner Club — Rachel Kahan, Lindsey Moore, and Anne Watters; the Eighth-grade Nerds — Therese Craparo and Amanda Scoblick; and the entire Gabel clan, whom I love.

Nola James had been standing on Weston Briggs's
cardboard-box-filled porch for ten minutes before real-
izing that she hadn't rung the doorbell. In fact, she
hadn't so much as moved since she'd climbed up the
steps and set her Skechers-clad feet on the dirty welcome mat. Nola wasn't sure if it was fear keeping her
from making her presence known or...Okay, it was
definitely fear. What made Nola think she could
develop some mean-spirited *Punk'd*-style plot against
her ex-best-friend-turned-nemesis Marnie, run next

door to the house newly occupied by Marnie's former boyfriend, and expect to go through with it?

Nola let out a heavy sigh, turned on her heel, and retreated a few paces. When she reached the edge of the porch, she turned her gaze upward and looked at the evening sky. The stars were twinkling above the city of Poughkeepsie like glitter, as a chilly autumn breeze kicked up piles of raked leaves in the yard. Nola zipped up her navy blue Columbia windbreaker and put her hands in her pockets, thinking about what she would do if she ever got up the nerve to ring that doorbell.

She'd concocted a basic three-pronged plan on the walk over here, which took her no more than thirty seconds. The first stage called for telling Weston that Marnie had just seen him from Nola's bedroom window and sent her out to ask him to meet her at Stewart's Ice Cream Shoppe tomorrow night. The second stage called for convincing Marnie to work on their English project together at Stewart's tomorrow after school. The third stage called for lurking outside of Stewart's to watch a stunned Marnie come face-to-face with Weston, the boy who threw her heart into a wood-chipper last year (metaphorically speaking, of course).

However, two of the three stages involved trickery, and that seemed to be everyone else's specialty but

Nola's. She was terrible at being deceitful and always cracked under the pressure. Actually, Nola could recall about twenty different instances (including one involving Marnie, stolen thongs, and a sales clerk at Victoria's Secret) when her back was against the wall and she had to tell a half-truth, only to be betrayed by her quivering bottom lip and her infamous hive outbreaks.

*This is ridiculous. There's no way I can pull this off.*

Suddenly the porch light flicked on and Nola's breath caught in her throat. She turned around and saw Weston Briggs in the door frame, smirking as if he'd just caught Nola coming out of the shower with only a towel wrapped around her.

"I'm not one-hundred-percent sure, but I think you're trespassing," he said.

While Nola never understood why Marnie was so hung up on Weston, now that she was standing less than ten feet away from him, she could see what all the fuss was about. Even though he was wearing a ratty orange baseball jersey and a dingy pair of jeans, Weston was the spitting image of Heath Ledger after batting practice. His blond hair was damp with perspiration and his big blue eyes were focused intensely on Nola, which made her extremely self-conscious. She hadn't even bothered to put on any lip gloss before she left her house. Not that it mattered what

Weston thought of her. After all, Nola was a girl on a mission (except at the moment the only thing she could remember about the mission was that it had prongs).

"So, Nola, are you going to tell me why you're here, or am I going to have to guess?" Weston asked as he strutted onto the porch and shut the door behind him.

Nola steadied herself and swallowed hard. She couldn't act nervous or Weston might suspect that she was up to no good. "I came to welcome you to the neighborhood."

Weston moved a stray box out of his path with his foot. "You live around here?"

"Right next door actually," Nola said, gesturing to her large, but quaint Victorian house, which appeared rather ominous in the dark.

"Small world," he said flatly. "Did you bring a basket of cookies or something?"

Nola let out a huff. *Small world? Basket of cookies?* Weston had dated Marnie for four whole months and *this* was the kind of response she got after he hadn't seen her for almost year? Nola hadn't expected a bear hug, but still.

"All I have is gum," she said as she pulled out a pack of cinnamon Trident out of her jacket pocket.

"Cool, thanks," Weston said, snatching it out of her hand.

*What the Hell? Why did Marnie give this guy the time of day?*

Weston took a piece of gum out of its wrapper and placed it ever-so-seductively on his tongue.

*Never mind.*

"So why did your family move back to Poughkeepsie?" Nola asked, hoping this would keep her from ogling Weston as he chewed.

"Eh, you know how it is," he said with a shrug.

Nola was completely baffled. "Yeah, I guess."

"How's Marnie doing?"

Nola gulped. This was the perfect opportunity to launch her scheme, which thankfully came flooding back at the mention of Marnie's name. However, as Weston continued to chomp on *her* Trident, Nola began to have second thoughts. Sure, Marnie deserved to be shoved off her self-righteous pedestal after everything she'd done to Nola—ditching her for Lizette Levin and her crew of mindless Majors, accusing Nola of vandalizing her posters, and baiting her into a tigress-fight at that stupid party on Saturday night, to name just a few evil things. But if Nola put this sneaky plan into motion, wouldn't she be sinking to Marnie's level?

Filled with doubt, Nola peered down at her sneakers and mumbled, "She's okay."

Weston chuckled. "I gotta admit. I'm surprised you two are still friends."

Nola's head snapped up. "What do you mean?"

"I know how you girls used to fight about me," Weston said with a wink. "*You* think I'm a dumb jock and a heartbreaker, huh?"

Nola could feel all of her appendages going numb. Back when Marnie first started going out with Weston, she and Nola had gotten into some low-grade spats over Weston's lack of smarts. Nola had also warned Marnie several times that he seemed kind of shady and would probably do her wrong, but Marnie never listened. Apparently, she'd never kept her mouth shut, either! How could Marnie sell Nola out like that even *before* Lizette Levin came on the scene?

*That's it. Marnie Fitzpatrick is going down. AND HARD!* "As a matter of fact, I do," Nola said, putting her hands on her hips in an attempt to steady herself. "But that's not important. When Marnie saw you from my bedroom window a few minutes ago, she was sobbing. She's still not over you, Weston."

He dashed over to the side of the porch, leaned on the railing, and glanced up in the direction of Nola's window. "Really? She's *crying*?"

Nola grinned. "Like a colicky baby."

"I just saw your curtains move. She must be watching me," Weston crowed.

*Wait a minute. Nobody should be in my room.*

Nola hightailed it over to Weston and peered up at her bedroom window. Not only did the curtains move again, but the light also switched off. At first, Nola thought that her little brothers Dennis and Dylan might have been playing hide-and-seek in there, but when she cast her eyes on the kitchen window she could see the both of them flinging food at each other with their spoons. That left one other person.

Ian Capshaw, Vassar College freshman and the James's family nanny.

"Wow, I had no idea Marnie was so…obsessive," Weston said, impressed.

"Yeah, me neither," Nola murmured. *What was Ian doing in my room?*

Weston ran his hands through his hair and took a whiff of his baseball jersey. "Maybe I should go over to your place and say hi."

Nola ripped her thoughts away from Ian and forced herself to stay on course. "Actually, Marnie wanted me to ask if you'd meet her tomorrow night at Stewart's. She really wants to see you…and treat you to some gelatos, if you know what I mean."

"I think I can swing that." Weston smiled widely.

"Great," Nola replied as she tucked her brown hair behind her ears and took another glimpse at her window.

*Now on to stage two.*

Five minutes later, Nola was flying around her room, making sure none of her high-risk personal items had been disturbed. Thankfully, her old fashioned, but broken (yikes!) lock-and-key diary was safely tucked inside an decrepit Connect Four box at the far reaches of her closet, and her yellow Mead five-subject notebook with all the *Matthew Thomas Heatherly*s written on the back cover was in her overstuffed Jansport, which was on the floor near her bed—exactly where she'd left it.

Nola breathed a small sigh of relief and sat down on her desk chair, zapped of all her energy. However, she felt a sharp pain rise in her chest when she realized that her computer was on. What if Ian had been reading her e-mails? Not that there was anything scandalous lurking in her in-box, but still—a teenage girl has to protect her right to privacy at all costs, especially when it's being invaded by a pain-in-the-neck seventeen-year-old male babysitter!

Nola held her breath when she jiggled her mouse and her kitschy Hannah Montana screen saver dissipated to reveal her e-mail account. Everything seemed in order, except that one new message had arrived.

*To: Nola James*
*From: Matt Heatherly*
*Subject: Forgive me?*

Even though she'd been both really worried and annoyed by Matt's sudden disappearance over IM and his absence at school today, Nola could feel her body go limp at the sight of his name. Luckily, the e-mail hadn't been opened. Otherwise, she might have gone berserk and kicked Ian out of the house.

Nola put one hand on her heart and used the other to double-click.

*Hey Nol,*

*Sorry about leaving you hanging yesterday. I wish I had a good excuse, but honestly, I'm very...confused. There is a reason behind it and I will tell you soon. I just can't explain everything right now. I hope you understand, and that you're not angry, because the truth is, you really mean the world to me.*

*Matt*

Nola stared at Matt's e-mail for so long she almost went into a meditative state. *You really mean the world to me? I just can't explain everything right now? I'm very confused?* Did all of this mean Matt was finally coming around and seeing her as more than just a friend?

Nola rubbed at her eyes and then looked at the screen again. Yep, the words were still there and this wasn't a hallucination. Maybe tomorrow Matt would ride over to her house on his bike, take her to Sunset Lake on the Vassar campus for a picnic breakfast, and profess his true feelings for her! Or maybe he'd write Nola a love song this time and show up on her doorstep to sing it to her. Nola's pulse was racing as she thought of all the romantic possibilities.

"Are you busy?" a voice came from behind her.

Nola swiveled around in her desk chair and saw Mr. Nosey McSnoops-a-lot standing out in the hall.

*God, why didn't I at least close my door?*

"Yes, I am," Nola said curtly, crossing her arms in front of her chest.

Ian marched into her room without even bothering to ask if he was welcome. "This will only take a second."

Nola gave Ian a frosty glare. *Is this the same boy that was actually being nice to me earlier?*

"So, that guy next door. What's his deal?" Ian

narrowed his eyes at Nola and tossed her a conde-scending look.

"His *deal*? What business is that of yours?" Nola's voice was crackling with anger. How dare Ian talk to her like this?

Ian rolled his eyes. "I'm in charge when your parents aren't home, remember?"

As Nola stood up, she felt her face turn hard. She had almost summoned up the courage to knock off the enormous chip Ian had on his shoulder when this goofy smirk appeared on his face.

"What's so funny?" she barked.

"Hannah Montana?" Ian replied with a chuckle. "How…*cute*."

Immediately, Nola's I-pity-the-fool-who-snoops-in-my-room mojo vanished into thin air.

*Ugh. It figures.*

"Are you through humiliating me now?" Nola muttered as she shuffled over to her bed and flopped onto her back.

Ian moved a few steps closer so he towered over Nola. Although she was completely irritated, Nola couldn't get over how good-looking Ian was. His eyes kind of sparkled when he was being mean and the smug expression that was permanently etched on his face oftentimes made him seem…irresistibly hot. Not that Nola would ever admit this under oath or anything. In fact, she would rather go to jail for committing perjury.

"Listen," Ian said with resigned sigh. "I'm just doing what I'm paid to do—keep an eye on the kids. Now, what's that guy's name and what were you two doing before?"

Nola sprang up from her bed so fast Ian jumped back a few feet. "I am *not* a little kid!" she growled.

Nola would have stopped there, but Ian looked as though he was about to laugh rather than apologize for being such a jerk. It was more than Nola could stand. "If you must know, his name is Weston and we were talking about *what a big loser you are*! Satisfied?"

Then something shocking happened. Ian's eyes dimmed and his pompous grin transformed into this hurt frown. He just stood there, gaping at Nola until he shook himself out of his daze and walked past her briskly.

Nola swallowed hard. She'd gone way too far. "Ian, wait. I—"

"Sorry I was spying before. It won't happen again," he said, before shutting the door quietly behind him and leaving Nola to wonder who she was turning into.

# To Do List: Read All the Point Books!

## By Aimee Friedman

- ☐ South Beach
  0-439-70678-5

- ☐ French Kiss
  0-439-79281-9

- ☐ Hollywood Hills
  0-439-79282-7

## By Abby Sher

- ☐ Kissing Snowflakes
  0-545-00010-6

## By Hailey Abbott

- ☐ Summer Boys
  0-439-54020-8

- ☐ Next Summer: A
  Summer Boys Novel
  0-439-75540-9

- ☐ After Summer: A
  Summer Boys Novel
  0-439-86367-8

- ☐ Last Summer: A
  Summer Boys Novel
  0-439-86725-8

## By Claudia Gabel

- ☐ In or Out
  0-439-91853-7

- ☐ Loves Me, Loves Me Not:
  An In or Out Novel
  0-439-91854-5

## By Nina Malkin

- ☐ 6X: The
  Uncensored
  Confessions
  0-439-72421-X

- ☐ 6X: Loud, Fast,
  & Out of Control
  0-439-72422-8

- ☐ Orange Is the New
  Pink
  0-439-89965-6

## By Pamela Wells

- ☐ The Heartbreakers
  0-439-02691-1